I0685603

ABERRATION

FEATURING STORIES BY

JAMES A. HUNTER   MELISSA KOONS

THOMAS A. FOWLER EMILY GODHAND

EDITED BY MELISSA KOONS

Aberration
Copyright 2018 Write Illusion LLC
ISBN Paperback: 978-1-7324422-4-5
ISBN eBook: 978-1-7324422-5-2
All rights reserved. No part of this publication may be reproduced, distributed, or transmitted in any form without the prior written permission of the author and/or publisher. This is a work of fiction. Although every precaution has been taken to verify the accuracy of the information contained herein, the author and publisher assume no responsibility for any errors or omissions. No liability is assumed for damages that may result from the use of information contained within.
Cover art designed by Thomas A. Fowler
www.nerdythingspublishing.com
Formatting designed by Spine Press + Post
www.writeillusionllc.com
www.spinepressandpost.com

TABLE OF CONTENTS

CONTENTS SUMMARY

"Mr. Flysuit and the Mandela Effect"
In nowhere's ville Wyoming, a group of reckless, young teenagers make the deadly mistake of accepting a dare that never should have been uttered. Being fourteen, they thought they could survive whatever the house at the edge of the cemetery could hold. They could never have anticipated the unexplained horrors that changed their lives forever.

"Last Bus to Brooklyn"
A detective working the graveyard shift in Brooklyn has seen his fair share of horrors. He's seen good men break under the pressure of nightmarish crimes the city throws at them. It's not a problem for him, except for one case. For decades, he's been tracking one murderer across the city, unable to find closure. Unsolved cases haunt him as the dreaded serial killer, Anubis, claims another victim.

"Penned in Gall"
A summer house party seems innocent enough, but capturing the attention of the beautiful host becomes an afterthought once a room that shouldn't exist is discovered. What the room houses and what it unleashes transform this house party into a nightmare.

"Brilliant Monstrosity"
A plain, young woman escaping her past and rural community flees to a bustling college town where she meets a striking and brilliant scientist. Determined to alter people's brain chemistry to cure anxiety conditions, the scientist and her modest assistant accidentally stumble upon a deadly discovery.

"Esophageal Foreign Body"

What starts off as a trip to the ER for a piece of improperly chewed diner transforms into a horrific discovery of an entirely different foreign body.

"All Yours"

Sailors are superstitious, knowing that they are at the mercy of the sea. One young sailor is about to discover that not all legends are fiction. Safe passage comes at a steep price.

"Germline Enhancement"

Curing cancer seems like it would be an act for the betterment of humanity. When the cure lies in altering genetic code, it comes at the cost of humanity.

"Reconciling the Dragon"

There is a nature within us. A nature that is deep and primal. As we age, we condition ourselves to suppress our primal beast but it's always there. Only the truly sane or deeply mad can master the reconciliation of the primal id and social ego.

"Sedated"

Detective Fumero knows that there is a connection behind the young women going missing in her city. The higher ups don't want to acknowledge the obvious: human trafficking. As Fumero pulls at the connecting thread between the missing women, her whole system and security begins to unravel. There's a reason she wasn't meant to solve this case.

"Follow Your Heart"

There is a hole in the last few hours of his mind. Left with an anxious feeling, Daniel works his way through his memories, searching for the missing time that has led him to the kitchen table and an unknown fear of what lurks beyond the bedroom door.

INTRODUCTION

Aberrations depart from the normal, bringing an unwelcome presence. They extract any sense of comfort away from our everyday lives. Their disruptions refuse to let you separate what is real. They take hold of our nightmares in an inescapable release from your own mind.

"Aberration" is the unsettling, the abnormal, the unusual. This anthology features ten stories from four authors. Each story explores the horrific themes of the abnormal and unsettling. Read of real monsters that do more than go bump in the night, and of monsters within that are just as terrifying.

"Aberration" will take you through a journey of horrors and thrills—each different from the last. Delve into the abnormal, the macabre, and the horrific. Experience what happens when aberrations, both surreal and abnormal, take hold and never leave you in these ten tales of horror. Edited by Melissa Koons, descend into a world disrupted. Descend into Aberration.

MR. FLYSUIT AND THE MANDELA EFFECT

JAMES A. HUNTER

There's this thing—a phenomena, really—called the "Mandela Effect."

This lady, Fiona Broome, coined the phrase back in 2010 and it's some bat-shit crazy stuff, lemme tell you what. See, Fiona Broome swears up, down, and sideways that Nelson Mandela died some time back in the 1980s while imprisoned in South Africa. And she's not alone. She, and a whole slew of other people claim to remember details about Mandela's funeral, including alleged CNN news coverage and even a scuffle over publishing rights involving Mandela's widow, Winnie.

But here's the wonky thing: none of that happened. None of it. Zero.

Mandela was freed from prison in February of 1990, went on to serve as President of South Africa from '94 to '99, and didn't pass away until 2013. So, Ms. Broome is wrong. They're *all* wrong. Every last one of the thousands of people who remember Mandela's prison death. Wrong. Wrong.

Wrong. It's a fact. Yet, these folks insist that it isn't; they insist Nelson Mandela died in the 1980s. They hold onto it like a religious creed, which is both fascinating and bizarre. And stranger still, more people are "remembering" this sequence of events all the time—it's like a disease, spreading around the internet, infecting minds and memories.

And thus, the Mandela Effect was born. Or maybe discovered.

Now, this would be weird enough, except there are other, similar, instances. Lots of them.

There are loads of people who believe in the existence of a 1990s movie called "Shazaam," where Sinbad plays a genie. Except that doesn't exist either. There's no film footage, no studio invoices (and there's *always* a paper trail), no reviews, and Sinbad's gone on record stating unequivocally that it never happened. Period. The end. But it's not the end because people still *believe*—despite all evidence to the contrary—it happened. They can't seem to get the notion out of their collective heads'. Then, there's the Berenstain Bears—or is it Berenstein Bears?—controversy. And Billy Graham's televised funeral, even though he's still alive (2017). And what about Curious George? Tail or no tail? Or Jif Peanut Butter vs. Jiffy Peanut Butter (hint, it's always and forever been Jif).

There's an enormous Reddit forum entirely dedicated to the Mandela Effect, with more topics and more examples if you're interested in seeing the weirdness of the internet in all its glory.

Now, some experts say the Mandela effect is a mass delusion; a false memory somehow contracted by thousands of people all at once. A type of collective misremembering. But there are other theories, too. Some people claim the Mandela effect is evidence of time-travel. No joke. They believe someone from the future went back and altered the past, creating these odd little ripples in time. Maybe, someone *saved* Mandela, causing the Berensteins to be replaced by their doppelgangers, the Berenstains, and poor Curious George ended up losing his tail—*shwick* gone. It's the Butterfly Effect played out in the minutia of life; just these little innocuous tweaks here and there.

Maybe that's it. Maybe not.

Ms. Broome, well she claims the Mandela Effect is the result of parallel universes—ones slightly off-kilter from our own—interacting. Rubbing shoulders while passing in the hallways of the cosmos or maybe slamming together on the subatomic level. Personally? That's the way I lean. But what the hell do I know? I'm not an expert. I've never gone to college, and I work at a crappy security booth making minimum wage.

Okay, so if I'm not some diploma-wielding "expert" why do I bring all this up?

I'll tell you why, because I've experienced the Mandela Effect, too. It's not some big internet-breaking meme like the Berenstain Bears or Sinbad the *not*-genie. It's smaller. More specific. More intimate. But if the fucking Mandela Effect *is* real, then this is it in spades. It has to be because I don't know how else to explain it. My Mandela Effect has to do with the house on the end of North Cedar, and I *know* it's real because the place almost fucking killed me. And it did kill Jackie Morgan and Mark Leaman. That's a fact.

Murdered them both, though it all got blamed on train accident.

It wasn't a train accident, though. Not by a country mile.

Okay, okay, let's roll things back a skoosh.

7

I grew up in Lusk, Wyoming.

It's this little dirt-speck town of maybe 1,500 people, sandwiching the US 85 like two pieces of stale bread, rotting from age. It's the kind of place that hardly warrants map space. The kind of place people drive through, but only because they're headed somewhere better, cleaner, nicer. Lusk has lots of old brick buildings—remnants from a different era—run-down motels, shitty glass-fronted diners, and even shittery gas stations/truck stops. Every vehicle in town is liable to be a pick-up; all of them old, rusted-out, and, of course, American made. It's a Podunk town, full of cowshit covered farmers, bored-ass rednecks, and wrinkleskinned retirees.

With all that said, there is one interesting thing about Lusk: and that's the house at the end of North Cedar past Jefferson Street, all the way at the edge of the cemetery.

It's an old dilapidated American Foursquare, perched on top of a small rise, snuggled back among a cluster of dark pines and leafy oaks. I can still see it perfectly in my head, just like an old photo. The sprawling front porch, framed by squat, square columns. The boards all worn and slightly warped. The white paint, stained and peeling. Dull windows running along the front, both upstairs and down, staring at the world like the menacing eyes of some giant spider. And it had this kooky weathervane on top—an antique brass rooster, riddled with green pockmarks—jutting up like a giant middle finger to the world. That damned weathervane always stands out in my mind.

Anyway, the place scared the absolute holy bejesus out of me as a kid.

Me and my pals, Jackie Morgan, Caroline Buckner, Mark Leaman (we called him Scooter), and Danny Carlisle, we'd go riding by it sometimes. We'd do it on a lark, just tearass past, pedaling our bikes a million miles a fucking hour, sure that something would burst out from beneath the front porch. Either that or come barreling out the front door, jaws yawning wide, yellow claws raking at the air, ready to disembowel the lot of us. I don't know why we thought that. No one lived there—the place was vacant and perpetually empty—and we'd never seen anyone go in or out. But the thought, the fear, persisted nonetheless.

All of that is to say, I remember that house in razor-sharp detail. And I remember what happened there, back in June of '95—and it did happen, God's honest truth.

It was the second week of summer break when we went in for the first time. And for the last, I suppose. We were having a sleepover—a "camping trip" technically—at Caroline Buckner's place, which was off of 4th and Holly by the elementary school. It's weird thinking back to that. I mean, we were all fourteen—except Danny, who was fifteen, held back a year because he was a fucking retard—and we were still doing co-ed sleepovers.

That's the mid-90s for you, though. None of our parents cared about Jack-shit as long as there was a modicum of supervision, and *technically* Caroline's dad was there. In reality, Caroline's dad was a full-blown alcoholic who was black-out drunk ninety-five percent of the day, so we were on our own. We could've been running trains back there, and that jackass wouldn't have noticed.

I mean we didn't, 'cause Caroline was basically one of the guys, but we totally could have.

What we did do, though, was steal a bottle of Vodka—it's fuzzy in my head, but I'm pretty sure it was Crown Russe—and got shitty drunk around a big ol' campfire. The booze tasted like paint thinner mixed with nail polish remover, but I remember drinking the holy-living crap out of it anyway. Burned my throat going down and left my eyes watering like I'd sliced a whole bag of onions, but I took slug

9

after slug like a champ. All of us did. We stood around, smoking stale Reds (also stolen), bathing in a drifting cloud of blue-gray smoke, while we cracked jokes and told ghost stories in the flickering firelight.

Some of the stories were classic urban legend fare: the Clown Statue, Bloody Mary, The Hook. Oldies but goodies, one and all.

Scooter told a couple of stories from that book, *Scary Stories to Tell in the Dark*. I still remember "Wonderful Sausage" and "The Red Dot." And Scooter was a helluva storyteller. He had a real knack for it. Knew exactly how to pace things, how to hit all the cues just right and string you along like some gullible sucker at a used car lot. He did this thing, where he'd drop his voice real low, so you'd have to crane your neck to hear, then *boom* an explosion of noise or a clap of his hands, and suddenly you were on a one-way trip straight to Scare-City. But, those stories were all bullshit, and we knew it.

Even in the dark, alone, with the Wyoming wilderness at our backs, we weren't scared.

Not really.

Not until Jackie told us his story about the house at the end of North Cedar.

"I've got a story," he'd said, his brown eyes downcast, his shoulders slumped, his mousy body curled in on itself while he smoked.

He'd gone in, not so long ago.

Decided to check it out after he heard some seniors from Niobrara County talking about how there was all kinds of booze and cigarettes stocked piled in the basement like rations squirreled away for the fucking Apocalypse. Loads and loads of old Whiskey and homemade moonshine. Good stuff, not like the swill we were drinking that night. So, Jackie went. Broke in through the back door, then trekked down into

10

the gloomy basement all by his lonesome. But there hadn't been any liquor waiting for him down there. Nope. Instead, there'd been a hole in the wall, beneath the basement stairs by the water-heater.

Inside that hole had been a man, or maybe not a man— Jackie seemed undecided about that. He wore old rags, this creep. Layers and layers of heavily stained coats and dirt-caked jeans. He looked like the most down-and-out Hobo Jackie had ever laid eyes on.

And if that weren't enough weirdness, he wore pelts, too, all stitched together like a cape. Rabbit skins, stained with old blood and gore. Bits of antler and yellowed bone attached with on leather straps. His skin was ashy, Jackie said, and withered like a worm left out in the sun. At first, Jackie had genuinely thought the guy was dead. Laying in that hole in the wall, unmoving and stiff as an old board. But when Jackie backed away, making for the stairs like any rational human being would, the guy shot right up.

His eyes wide, back arched, arms rigid.

Jackie wasn't an idiot, so he didn't wait around to bullshit with the weirdo. Nope. No way.

He bolted for the stairs like an Olympic track star, legs pumping as fast as they'd carry him. He was most of the way up when the pounding started. *Thump-thump-thump-thump-thump*. A pair of fists beating furiously against the underside of the wooden steps. When Jackie got to the top of the stairs, he faltered. *Run* his mind clambered at him, *run and don't ever look back*. But he *did* look back—it was a compulsion too strong to resist. A bit like watching an oncoming car accident: you know it's gonna be fucked, but you just can't seem to look away.

Well, Jackie looked, just a quick gander over one shoulder, and honestly, I can't blame him. How often have I slogged up the stairs late at night, but then paused to look back down—to reassure myself some snarling beast isn't tearing after me?

It's instinct. Nature.

The man, loaded down with pelts, waited at the landing, one skeletal finger outthrust in accusation. Jackie lingered, fascinated and horrified in equal parts, his legs suddenly unwilling to cooperate or carry him any farther. The man-thing canted his head to one side, rheumy eyes squinting, and opened his mouth. At first, there were no words, just this long, building *screech* like a bag full of cats stuck in a cement mixer—Jackie's words, not mine. It was a sound no human could ever make. Still, Jackie stood transfixed. Watching. That screech, it built and built, rising in a terrible crescendo, slowly morphing into actual words:

"LET ME IN! LET ME IN! LET ME IN! LET ME IN!"

The words were a constant stream, screamed from a thousand different voices all at once, each one slightly out of key with the other, but all coming from the same mouth. That awful racket, it seemed, finally broke the strange spell rooting Jackie in place. He turned, darted into the foyer, and right out the front door like Hell was on his heels.

Jackie shrugged when he finished telling us the story, then ran a trembling hand through his sandy blond hair. He tried to play it cool, but he failed—he was scared, and we could all see it. "Probably just some hobo hitching on the rails," he'd said after a time.

That was possible.

It wasn't unheard of for Hobos to occasionally stopover in Lusk for a day or two, since the Union Pacific Rail Line curved just north of town and south of the cemetery. We all bobbed our heads in agreement, but we also edged closer to the fire because none of us believed it.

The "Red Dot" might've been bullshit, but this was something different. We all felt it in the gut, I think. This was a *real* thing, a confirmation of something we'd always believed deep down. Sometimes, I wonder if our belief is what opened the door to that Hellhole in the first place. Doesn't really matter, I suppose. We were quiet for a while, smoking our cigarettes, passing around the cheap Vodka, all the fun ghost-stories discarded and done away with like spent party favors. Everyone was shaken, but okay, right up until that moron Danny fucktard Carlisle had to go and open his drunk, idiot mouth.

If anyone should've died in there, it should've been him.

After all these years, I can still hear Danny's voice echoing around the campfire, his words slightly slurred and blurred on the edges. "Holy shit guys, let's fucking go there." He swayed drunkenly on his leather, shit-kickers. "I think Jackie's full of cowpies. His eyes are turnin' brown from all the horseshit he's spoutin'. So, I say we call him out. Go over to that dump and march right down to the basement. And if there is some hobo"—he sneered and grabbed his crotch in a *fuck-em* gesture.

No one wanted to go, of course.

We all felt the weight of Jackie's story, the uneasiness of his words.

But we were young, dumb, and full of cum, and even more importantly we were full of cheap Vodka. Way, way, way too much cheap Vodka. Fucking Crown Russe. Besides, even though no one wanted to go, no one wanted to say so and be singled out as a pussy. Even Caroline, who legitimately *had* a pussy, didn't want to get slapped with that moniker. Shit, if anything, she was even more go-hung, eager

13

to prove she was braver than any dick-swinging dude in our crew.

So, like the teenage idiots we were, we went.

None of us had a car, so instead, we loaded up on our bicycles—a mix of Treks, Huffies, and vintage Schwinns—and peddled our drunk asses across town, sticking to the dusty back roads to avoid getting caught, and up to that god-forsaken house at the end of North Cedar. It was dark as the heart of the ocean when we got there. The moon, a sickly thumbnail of silver hanging in the sky, was so obscured by rolling clouds it was as useless as tits on a helicopter. We had camping flashlights, though. Big, ol' yellow sonsabitches that required a battery as big as a baseball to run.

Danny was the first one to turn his on, cutting through the deep, cemetery gloom with the yellow beam.

The house looked the same as it always did—same boxy columns, same chipped paint, same dull windows—except now, the front door was open. Waiting for us. Just a crack, understand, showcasing a thin crease of inky black. But it *was* fucking open. If there'd been one brain cell between the whole lot of us, we would've turned back right that second, and screwed youthful pride right up its ass. But here's the thing about being young: you think you'll live forever. Everything's a joke and a dare because nothing bad can happen to a fourteen-year-old.

Not anything really bad. Like death.

"Let's do this shit," Danny said, overflowing with false bravado, cracking his knuckles like he was getting ready to wade into a fistfight instead of the mouth to Hell.

"Yeah," I replied with a nod, trying not to sound like a colossal piece of chicken-shit.

"Does that mean you're volunteering to go first?" Scooter asked, his gaze shifting nervously between me and the barely-open door. His question hung in the air; every eye was fixed on me, expectant for my answer. *You a pussy, dude?* Those stares inquired. *You all talk, or do you got the balls to back it up?*

"Yeah, obviously," I replied with a sniff and an eyeroll. "It's just a shitty old house. And if there is some crackhead hobo?" I paused, bent over, and picked up a rusty piece of rebar laying on a pile of loose scree. "I'll fucking show him what's what." With the rebar in one hand and my square flashlight in the other, I soldiered forward, leaving the others to trail behind me. I took a deep breath and trudged up the steps; the old wood bowed under my weight, letting out soft moans and groans as though the house were a living thing. I flashed the light across the windows, but the curtains—dreary yellowing things—were closed tight, obscuring the interior.

I used the length of rebar to nudge the door open, sweeping my beam into the foyer.

A fine layer of dust, recently disturbed by the passage of feet, Jackie, probably, covered the hardwood floors, which were heavily scuffed and stained. Floral wallpaper—bubbled, deeply cracked, and sporting more than a few splashes of graffiti—decorated the walls. I inched into the room and swept my flashlight left; the beam washed over a boxy living room with the same tattered and peeling floral print. There was an old couch pushed up against the far wall; an ugly thing of faded orange and yellow fabric, which had to be from the 60s. Most of the cushions were slashed open, trailing white stuffing like gory ropes of intestine.

There was also a stained mattress in the center of the floor, covered in empty beer bottles and old piss stains, which reeked like the inside of a hot, Porta-John. The whole house smelled like that. Fucking gross.

Further on, connecting to the living room, was a square dining space with a great, big ol' table, which lay in pieces on the floor, all its legs ripped off and scattered. Nothing that way, either. I paused for a moment, stealing a peek over one shoulder at my friends who were lined up on the porch behind me, clustered together, looking small, pale, and frightened to their toes. "Come on," I said. "The stairs must be over that way"—I jerked my head toward the right and moved deeper into the house.

There was a kitchen up ahead, the floors covered in green linoleum. The few appliances that remained—a beat-to-shit gas stove and a drunkenly leaning fridge with the door hanging open—were so dusty I could tell they hadn't been used in ages. A lone chair, wooden and high-backed, sat in the middle of the room. There was a big staircase hugging the right wall, shooting up like an arrow, but I didn't see the stairs leading down.

There were two doors, though, situated between the kitchen and the staircase, and both were closed up nice and tight. I adjusted and readjusted my grip on the length of rebar—my palm slick and sweaty—and headed for the pair of doors.

The floorboards squeaked and squealed as my friends followed, completely silent except for their footfalls and the sound of heavy breathing. I padded closer to the pair of doors, a creeping dread building in my stomach and clawing up my throat like a bout of nausea. I pushed it down, determined not to pussy out.

Which door to pick was a coin-toss, so I tucked the flashlight beneath my armpit and pulled open the one on the left, closest to the kitchen. I let out a ragged sigh of relief as my light splashed over the interior of a small bathroom with a chipped clawfoot tub, a porcelain sink, and a broken mirror—the jagged pieces carpeting the floor. One down, one to go. I scooted over to the next door, this time hesitating, my hand quivering on the knob. Sweat broke out across my forehead, and my heart thumped like a jackhammer in my chest. More than anything in the world, I didn't want to open that door. I didn't want to go down into the basement and meet the hobo in the furs.

"What's the fuckin' holdup?" Caroline taunted from behind. "You lose your nerve, Mack? Maybe you need to grow a pair? Might be, I have some I could lend you"—she grabbed at her crotch. That earned a chorus of nervous, muted chuckles.

I absently flipped her the bird in reply, steeled myself, and yanked open the door, ready for a faceless monster to pounce.

The door whooshed out, but there was no monster waiting. No man, loitering at the foot of the stairs demanding I *let him in*. I took the wooden steps slowly, descending into the dark as the hairs on the back of my neck stood stiff. There were spaces between each step and I couldn't help but envision a pale white hand shooting out and wrapping around my ankle, clamping down like a vice, then dragging me away. But there was no hand or ankle grabbing, just like there'd been no murderous hobo.

The basement was gloomy and dank, but no creepier than the rest of the fucked-up house. Some old boxes—warped and moldy from the accumulated moisture—took up space against one wall and copper tubing, littered with spider-webbing, decorated the ceiling. There was a rusted, pot-bellied furnace, complete with an actual door for feeding in wood, in the left corner. Metal ductwork poked up from the furnace like gnarled fingers, disappearing into the ceiling. Beneath the stairs was the water heater, and just as Jackie had said, there was a jagged hole in the concrete next to it.

An artificial cave, six-feet high and four or five deep.

Tucked inside was a pallet made of old blankets, but no bum. There was, however, liquor. A shit-ton of bottles, some plastic, others glass. Wine, Whiskey, Vodka, Schnapps. Good stuff, too, though no smokes.

"Holy shit," Danny said, spotting the treasure-trove, "we hit motherfucking pay-dirt here." The others whooped and hollered, clapping each other on the shoulders in congratulations, the fear banished, replaced by adrenaline and greed. Jackie didn't look relieved, though. He looked even more anxious.

"Well, let's get the real party started," Scooter said, shoving past me and into the hole, pulling free a full bottle of Goldschlager. He held it up, giving it a swirl, the flecks of gold dancing and weaving in the beam of my flashlight.

We'd been drinking for maybe an hour when we heard the *clunk, clunk, clang* of something scraping and rooting around. It sounded like an animal, a big one. Everyone fell deathly silent, eyes going wide and wild as the sound came again. *Clunk, clunk, clang.* Louder this time. In the quiet, it wasn't hard to tell where the noise was coming from: the potbellied furnace in the corner. Everyone scrambled to their feet, beating a hasty retreat for the stairs as the sound grew louder and more persistent. Jackie was the first one up the stairs, his shoes thudding on the wood, followed by Caroline, Scooter, Danny, and me, bringing up the rear.

Everyone froze, though, as the handle on furnace firewood hatch *screeched* open, and the metal door swung outward with a rusty groan. My hands trembled—flashlight wavering, rebar twitching—as I stared at a square of pitch black, hardly large enough to accommodate a small child, in the center of the furnace. There was nothing there, though, and for a second I almost chalked it up to coincidence. Maybe

18

some sort of critter had gotten in. Like a possum or a large squirrel. But then a pallid face—completely bald, maggot white, and deeply creased like old boot leather—appeared in the opening.

A crude set of symbols were carved across its forehead, the wounds still red and puffy. After all these years, I can still see that damned symbol clear as day—like it's tattooed on my brain or something. I drew it out for anyone interested:

The breath caught in my throat and I thought I might vomit as the thing stared at me with milky, pink eyes. I would've said it was blind—how could it not be?—but then it winked at me, as though reading my thoughts, and offered me a sly lopsided smile. Its pencil-thin lips pulled back, revealing a mouth full of nubby, black teeth like pieces of broken glass. A tongue, chalky and white, slipped free, running around the edges of its too-wide mouth. Then, the creature—and I was sure as shit it was a creature and not a man—pulled itself from the furnace in the herky-jerky motions of bad stop-motion animation.

Spidery hands, tipped with dirt-caked nails, came first, attached to overlong arms as it wriggled and wormed its torso free. Its arms were bulky, as though it were wearing jacket after jacket, but it didn't take long to notice the "coats" were moving. *Shifting.* I gagged. Not coats, though that was an easy mistake to make at a glance. Flies. Millions of the black-bodied things. And over the top of those, were the pelts. Rough cut garments, crudely stitched together into a tattered cloak of fluttering trophies. There were patches of pale pink flesh—almost like dried, uncured pigskin—woven into that grotesque mantle.

One piece of leather, a little larger than my palm, had a faded tattoo on it: a pair of praying hands with a rosary looped around them like a noose.

"Holy fucking, McFuckerson!" Danny screamed from behind me, grabbing my shirt with a meaty palm and pulling me on. His words, bristling with unapologetic terror, seemed to jar everyone to frantic motion, and we all broke like a herd of stampeding cows. Unlike Jackie, I didn't pause when I reached the top; I didn't need to because I could hear the thing scrambling and skittering over the concrete floor, drawing ever-closer. I knew it hadn't made it to the stairs yet, but I could almost feel it reaching for me, its hot, fetid breath brushing up against the nape of my neck.

I darted through the entry; Danny promptly slammed the door shut behind me with a booming thunderclap.

"Get the fuck outta the way," Caroline hollered, sprinting toward us with the lone chair from the kitchen. I shuffled back, head reeling from what I'd just witnessed, as she crammed the chair up beneath the door knob. And not a moment too soon. The second she had it wedged firmly in place, the door handle rattled and shook, followed by a fist slamming against the wood. *Thunk-thunk-thunk.* I stared at the door, trapped and immobilized. Then, the creature shrieked, an inhuman noise like a buzzsaw cutting into a piece of sheet metal.

20

"LET ME IN! LET ME IN! LET ME IN! LET ME IN!"
"Let's go," Danny said, tugging on my shoulder. I didn't need much prompting. I wheeled around and beelined for the front door, except Scooter was already there, desperately turning the knob, trying to pry the door open. It didn't budge, not an inch. "The windows," I said, my voice oddly calm and detached, "bust 'em out."

Jackie was moving before the words were even out of my mouth, sprinting toward the windows in the living room. He threw back the musty yellow curtains, but faltered, confusion and fear dashing across his face in turns. It was easy to understand why. Instead of cloudy glass, staring out on the forlorn graveyard, there was simply a sheet of implacable wallpaper. Smooth and seamless, as though no windows had ever existed there. Caroline tried the windows near the stairwell leading to the second floor.

More of the same. Just blank walls, covered in that gaudy floral print.

Another crash from the basement doorway drew my eye. The creature was still shrieking its *let-me-in* hymn, but now it was working over the door like a boxer going to town on the heavy bag. The door rattled in its frame, the wood bowing and splintering with each successive blow. "Backdoor, and kitchen windows," I yelled at Jackie, "check 'em all. Everyone else ..." I paused, glancing around wild-eyed. "Weapons. Find a weapon. Anything you can defend yourself with." Everyone scattered, most heading for the living and dining rooms, while I made for the basement door.

Since I already had a weapon, and a decent one, I planted myself in front of the basement door, flashlight trained on the cracking wood, rebar raised and ready to go.

"It's the same back here," Jackie called out, scampering out of the kitchen, a pitted butcher knife clutched in one white-knuckled fist. "Door won't budge, and there aren't any windows." He spun in a slow circle like an animal trapped in a cage. "What are we gonna do, Mack? What the fuck are we gonna do?"

I shook my head because I didn't have an answer.

The others appeared a few seconds later, clutching an assortment of wooden table legs from the dining room and busted beer bottles from the piss-stained mattress in the living room.

"Alright, backdoor's fucked, too," I said, never taking my eyes off the basement stairwell. "Only way left to go is up."

"You fuckin' high?" Danny hissed. "Why would we go up? There's five of us, one of him, and we got weapons. Let's just bust this sumabitch up."

"Shut the fuck up, Danny!" I yelled, rounding on him. "That thing isn't human you fucktard—it's a monster. A demon or some shit. I dunno. And you don't even get a say because you're the only reason we're here. *'Let's fucking go there ... Jackie's full of cowpies.'* This is all your fault, jackass, now shut your mouth and get upstairs. Maybe the windows will work up there, and if not ... Well, maybe there's a way we can get to the roof."

Jackie and Caroline went without hesitation, but Danny and Scooter lingered, heading over to the living room, preparing to take a stand. "Don't be morons," I said, backtracking for the staircase, happy as a pig in shit to get away from that screeching—*"LET ME IN! LET ME IN! LET ME IN! LET ME IN!"*—playing on repeat like a broken record. I was a few feet from the staircase when the basement door exploded outward, chunks of wood flipping through the air like shrapnel. The thing from the basement didn't waste a second. Nope, it scuttled out on all fours like an overgrown, human-faced fly.

Mr. Flysuit, I thought deliriously.

"Let's get this fucker!" Danny screamed, charging in, a broken table leg upraised like a medieval mace while his flashlight beam bobbed and weaved. Scooter was a step behind. I rounded the stairs, but had to stop—*had to*—and watch. I honestly can't say why. Mr. Flysuit was skinny even with the layers of shifting flies carpeting its body, but it moved like a snake and hit like a Mac-Truck. Danny lashed out with his club, a wild swing, which sailed clear over the creature's head. The demon shot inside his guard and blasted him in the chest with a closed fist, lifting Danny into the air, flipping him ass over tea kettle.

He crashed in a heap not far off, limbs splayed out, eyes hazy from shock.

I hesitated, eyeing the stairs then Danny, the stairs then Danny.

Finally, I rushed over, helping the moron to his feet, glancing up in time to see Scooter lunge forward, thrusting a broken bottle toward the thing's face. Flysuit batted aside the attack with lazy ease, then leaped like a pitbull, nails slashing into Scooter's throat, drawing a deep line of red across the skin. Scooter dropped the bottle and staggered back, clutching his ruined neck, mouth wide as blood leaked between his fingers. Flysuit wasn't done. It tackled Scooter around the middle, driving a shoulder into his gut, and bringing him to the ground.

I tore my eyes away.

There was nothing we could do here. Not for Scooter. Maybe not for ourselves. Instead, I turned and dragged Danny up the stairs, pursued by the gut-wrenching sound of Mr. Flysuit chewing and slurping. There was another door at the top of the stairs, but Jackie and Caroline were gone. Vanished. Danny and I shoved our way through, leaving Scooter to die, guilt riding my back like a monkey.

The door swung shut, and darkness enveloped us, save for the meager illumination our flashlights provided. But there wasn't anything for our flashlights to illuminate. The room, if it was really a room, seemed to stretch on forever with no walls and no visible end. It was an impossibly big space, and there was no way to tell where we were or where we needed to go. There was no sign of Caroline or Jackie, either. Danny and I were lost in an ocean in the dead of night without any idea of where the shore lay.

"Where the fuck are we?" Danny asked in a harsh whisper, sweeping his light fruitlessly from left to right. "Where the fuck are we?" He said again, this time more to himself than to me.

I turned around, searching behind me for the door. I found the wall easily enough—covered in the same awful floral print as below—stretching off in either direction for as far as I could see, but there was no door. I turned again, pressing my back firmly against the wall, and shouted. "Jackie?!" I paused as my voice echoed and bounced, oddly distorted. "Caroline?!"

After a few long moments, Caroline answered. "We're here ... Near the door." Her voice sounded faded, weak, and impossible to pinpoint. It felt like hearing someone shout while under water. "Follow the wall," Jackie called. "But watch out for the ..." his words guttered and died, as though the house had silenced him before he could spoil whatever surprise it had in store for us.

"Jackie?! Caroline?!" Danny hollered, a hand cupped around his mouth. This time, there was no answer. Just crushing, terrible silence and all-pervading darkness.

24

"Come on," I said, nudging Danny in his meaty shoulder. I turned right and walked, trailing the length of rebar along the wall as I scanned the featureless room for any sign of Jackie, Caroline, or an exit. Danny walked behind me, checking our backtrail every few steps to make sure the freak from the basement wasn't tagging along behind us. I didn't see anything, but I felt eyes on my back the whole while, as if someone, or lots of someones, were watching us from just outside the range of my flashlight.

We walked for a long time, ten minutes maybe, when my light finally flashed over something up ahead: a corner, with another long wall angling off to the left.

Instead of celebrating at the find, though, I skittered to a stop. Danny ran into me from behind, "What the fuck ..." he started. His words cut short as his gaze landed on the boy standing ahead, head bowed, facing the corner like a toddler in time out. He was a dusky skinned black kid, maybe five, in thoroughly stained blue pajamas. The cuffs were ripped and frayed. I crept away on silent feet, driven by instinct, but stopped again when I heard the rustle of movement coming from behind me.

The noise was faint, barely-there at all. The scuttle and scrape of nails on the floor and the distant droning of flies.

The kid in the corner seemed to hear the sound, too, and turned his head toward us, the rest of his body stiff and unmoving. A scream built in my chest, but caught in my throat like a piece of popcorn; all that came out was a weak, hollow squeak. The boy had no face. It was like someone had used a giant ice-cream scoop to hollow out his entire skull, leaving only a sliver of chin and an edge of forehead as a reminder of what had once been. There was no blood, gore, or bone, though. And no strings of gray brain matter. Nope. Just a hollow cavity, filled with inky shadow.

The little kid lifted a finger, placing it where his mouth should've been. "Shhh," he hissed, despite not having a mouth. "He comes"—the scuttling intensified, the *scritch-scratch-scritch* drawing closer as the buzzing built—"and all will be punished." Then, the little boy simply turned back to the wall, resuming his self-imposed timeout.

"Fuck this shit," Danny said, shaking his head like he refused to believe his eyes. "We gotta go, Mack. We gotta go." He spun, not waiting for me to reply, and bolted away from the wall, running headlong into the darkness and not caring. Anything to get away from the creepy-ass kid without a face. I hesitated for only a heartbeat before taking off too, training my flashlight on Danny as we ran. This was dumb, I knew—we should've tried to skirt around the boy and follow the wall—but I couldn't stomach the thought of being stuck in here alone.

I saw nothing as I ran, just choking blackness and scuffed hardwood floors underfoot. But I heard the constant *scritch-scratch-scritch* of nails on wood the whole way. Eventually, a wooden door—the frame covered in jagged green script, pulsing with cancerous light—materialized out of the dark. Aside from the strange runes running along the frame, the door looked identical to the one we'd entered the room through. Except there were no walls around it. It stood free and unsupported like an ancient Egyptian obelisk. I slowed my mad dash, and circled it slowly, carefully, running my fingers over the surface as I walked.

It vibrated subtly beneath my digits, but didn't seem to lead anywhere. How could it?

When I tried the knob, though, it turned easily in my hand, swinging open, spilling a pool of dirty purple light across the floor. *What the fuck is this place?* I thought before hustling through—eager to leave the black room behind. The odd door deposited Danny and me in a new room, except it wasn't a "room" at all. It was a fucking forest is what it was. The ground a sea of lush green grass, the landscape peppered by towering oaks, old growth pines, and broad-leafed sycamores. And like everything else in this place, the forest wasn't natural.

The trees were wrong, for one: The leaves and pine needles were all varying shades of red. The tree trunks were twisted things that looked like human bodies, but distorted and broken, with faces protruding out—each permanently locked in a rictus of suffering. High above, a bloated purple moon hung in a cloudless sky like a rotten plum. Strangest of all, though, were the doors. More freestanding doors, haphazardly strewn among the trees. Each door was nearly identical: thick wood, scrolling runes, and a square window in the center. But each peered out on a different destination.

I saw a few towns—Podunk places, not so different from Lusk—and a handful of big cities with yawing skyscrapers of steel and glass. But there were other places, too. Fantastical, impossible places where the air burned, were islands floated unsupported in the sky, where creatures made of discarded branches, rotten vines, sludgy mud, and bits of bone, milled about in deep shadow.

None of those doors were ours, I knew—they might open for others, but not for us. There was only one door for us. One door which would lead back to Lusk and that was the one we needed to find. "Let's go," I said to Danny. "We need to find Jackie and Caroline if we can. Either that or the way out … If there is a way out," I finished weakly.

"Yeah," he mumbled softly, wheeling about, eyes wide as saucers.

We walked—walked for so long, I lost track of time. I was on the verge of giving up, sitting down, leaning back against one of the distorted body trees, and closing my eyes for a while, when Danny gave out a hoot of joy, pumping a fist in the air. Jackie and Caroline emerged from a thick cluster of pines not far ahead, stumbling around drunkenly, their faces pale, their movements languid. Even at a glance, I could tell they were exhausted to the bone, but they looked up at the sound of Danny's cry, huge smiles breaking across their faces almost in unison.

Those smiles slipped, though, falling by the wayside as they caught sight of something behind us. A creeping dread spread through me like a fever and I was suddenly sure the man with flies was behind us, silently creeping through the grass on all fours, ready to pounce. To maim. To kill. A cold sweat broke out along my forehead and trickled down my back. I clenched down on the spit of rebar and spun, lips pulled back in a snarl. Instead of the Mr. Flysuit, though, was the front door to the house at the end of North Cedar point.

And not just the door, the whole foyer. The floral-clad walls grew right up out of the ground as if they were a natural part of the landscape. Except now, a single phrase was gouged into the drywall over and over again: *Let Me Out.* The ragged edges of the lettering, combined with smears of dried brown, made me think those marking had been made by hand. Carved out with desperate, bloody fingers. I glanced down and noticed the floorboards were back, too, blending and bleeding seamlessly into the grass behind me—it was impossible to pinpoint where one ended, and the other began.

"We never should've come here," Jackie said, his normally mousy voice, certain and somber. "This is my fault. I knew it wasn't a hobo, but I told the story anyway. I started this." He clenched his jaw tight and marched forward, slipping between Danny and me and right up to the door. He extended a hand, but hesitated just inches from the knob. Unsure. Thinking back, it's almost like he knew what was coming, even though that's impossible. He nodded his head, then, as if accepting his fate, and clasped the knob, giving it a sharp turn.

This time, the door swung inward with a squeal, revealing the grassy rise and the cemetery beyond. Flysuit was also standing there, crouched low to the ground, its lips pulled back, revealing its broken-glass teeth. It shot forward, jabbing its talon-tipped fingers into Jackie's gut, plunging in and out, over and over again like a pair of meaty pistons. Jackie stumbled back, dropping his table-leg club, groping at his stomach while frothy crimson gurgled between lips. His heel caught on a rock, protruding from the ground, and he went down like a load of bricks.

Flysuit attacked like a shark with a nose-full of blood, scrambling onto Jackie, driving its bony knees into his ruined gut, clamping its jaws around his throat, while flies poured into Jackie's open mouth. Their writhing bodies choking off his cries. Caroline, Danny, and I had two options at that moment: attack the thing murdering our friend or run. Fight or flight, distilled down to its most basic form. Danny chose first, shoving past me as he lumbered for the door, terror in his eyes and Jackie already forgotten. I wish I could say I'd done something different, that I'd been braver. Better.

I wasn't. I hooked an arm around Caroline, frozen in place with indecision, and bolted.

I glanced back one last time as I'd cleared the front porch, and though it's hard to be certain, I could've sworn Flysuit loitered in the doorway, and behind him, was a new sapling sprouting up from the center of Jackie's sunken chest.

I don't remember how we got back to Caroline's. None of us did. We all woke up the next morning as the sun crept up over the horizon, shooting golden fingers into the pale blue sky. It almost felt like everything from the night before had just been a terrible nightmare, brought on by a combination of too much alcohol and too many cheesy campfire horror stories. Except we were two people short. Scooter and Jackie were gone, their bikes nowhere to be seen. A farmer—fella by the name of Lesly Hawthorn from Manville—found their bodies later that day, over by the tracks.

Hit by a Freight train then picked over by a pack of coyotes. I still have the article:

Okay, there it is—the story I haven't told a soul, not in twenty years. Now, let's get back to the present and back to the Mandela Effect. So, a couple of months ago, I returned to Lusk for my twenty-year high school reunion. I didn't go back for the ten-year, because I couldn't force myself to see the place again, not after what had happened. Couldn't stand to look my parents in the eye, to drive down the 85, or talk with the old crew, sans Jackie Morgan and Mark Leaman, obviously. I just couldn't do it. I didn't want the nightmares to come back.

But after twenty years? After twenty-years ... Well, I just threw my hands up and said fuck it. Fuck it all.

The town was more modern than I remembered, but only just. Mostly, it was the same shitty brick buildings, the same glass-fronted diners (a few had different names, at least), and the same sagging faces, even more tired and worn down by the years. Honestly, the place looked like it had one foot in the grave—one stiff breeze might've blown everything over and wiped the whole place right off the map good and proper. That probably wouldn't be a bad thing. Still, there was some part of me that felt *good* being there; going back was this cathartic experience, like I was finally ready to move past everything.

To *really* put it behind me.

Naturally, the first thing I did was putter on up to the house at the end of North Cedar in my Camry: the tires bald, the suspension shot, the front window cracked, a huge dent in the front fender. I headed north on 85 (South Cedar Street in town), cruising past a mom-and-pop drugstore and the Harald Newspaper building, then over the train tracks on the edge of the town proper. I veered left onto North Main Street—a two-lane cut of asphalt with a squat, white plaster propane shop on the right—and headed straight for another two-hundred feet, which saw me through the stone, cemetery gates.

I idled past the swath of green grass, studded with tombstones like blunt gray teeth, and into the pine trees on the far side. It didn't take me long to find the rise at the end of North Cedar, the one where the house should've been, but wasn't. I killed the car, unbuckled my seat belt, and slid out. I frowned, fished a pack of Reds from my pocket, and lit up a smoke as I leaned against the hood of my car. I stood there for a good half-an-hour, chain smoking cigarette after cigarette, my arms folded across my sunken chest, nicotine flooding my system, as I stared at the unassuming plot of land.

There was an old, concrete slab there, pitted and chipped. A foundation. Like maybe someone, years and years ago, had thought about building something out here, but finally decided against it. You can see that slab on Google maps if you're inclined to check (42.773047, -104.452130), but there wasn't any sign of the house. No sign of the basement either. It had been twenty years, so my assumption was someone had just leveled the damned place and backfilled the basement in with concrete. Except, that's not what happened.

It was the fucking Mandela Effect.

See, I climbed into my car and headed back into town, stopping at this cozy hole-in-the-wall for lunch.

I ordered a greasy burger and made idle small talk with a tired-looking waitress with a wave of chestnut hair, going gray at the temples, and deep bags under her eyes. Eventually, I asked her about the house at the end of North Cedar, the one past Jefferson Street by the cemetery. She'd been in Lusk almost as long as I'd been away, but she'd never heard of the place. Not a once. Not even as part of some scary, local urban legend. I smiled, thanked her, and finished my meal in peace. After that, I made a pit stop at a gas station, asking a pudgy kid of maybe nineteen about the house.

Same question, same answer.

The Harald Newspaper was open, so I stopped there next. James Mackerson—a bean pole with a basset-hound face, who'd run the Harald even when I'd been a kid—was tooling around the office. The guy had to be in his early seventies, but he was still working hard, and looking pretty damned spry for such an old fella. He didn't remember me (not that I offered him my name), but even more disconcerting, he didn't remember the house. He insisted no such place had ever existed. Just that stone pad, laid out in the 1940s, by a pair of brothers named the McClains.

No one remembered.

No one, except Caroline Buckner.

Jackie and Scooter were dead, and Danny was long gone—in prison from what I could find—but Caroline was at the reunion.

She hadn't aged well. Her body had gone soft and flabby, her hair prematurely gray; not that I was in a position to cast stones. I looked like a giant bag full of soggy dicks. Still, I knew it was her in an instant. I could tell by her steely blues eyes and the lines of her jaw. And one look at her told me all I needed to know: she remembered, alright. The way she tensed up when she saw me: the wild, panicked look in her gaze followed by a wave of guilt sprinting across her features. I didn't need to ask because the memories were carved into her flesh like old scars. I did ask, though, because I'd come from Milwaukee for this and I needed to be sure.

Needed it more than I've ever needed anything else.

Our conversation was brief; neither of us could stomach talking about what happened in the house, I think. But she remembered, and maybe even more importantly, she also told gave me a few names—people like us who knew about the house, too. Brian Wilkerson, this guy a couple of years older than us, who went to Niobrara County High. Jamie Burakoff, a soccer mom from Manville who dated this high school buddy of mine, Chad Jenkins. Not a lot of people, but enough people to reinforce that I wasn't bat-shit bonkers.

The motherfucking Mandela Effect, am I right?

I mean, I *know* that place is real. I'm not crazy.

And Mr. Flysuit? I *know* he's real, too. Know it as sure as I know the sky is blue. Him, I still see. Not always, not even often, but sometimes. In a pocket of deep shadow. Or as a blur, just out the corner of my eye. Sometimes there's a flash of him in my mirror, or in my computer screen late at night. I see his face, distorted and indistinct, mouthing the words *let me in, let me in, let me in.* He's already got his hooks into me. Not enough to break through from wherever he lives, but enough for me to get a glimpse of him whenever our universes rub shoulders from time to time.

I wonder sometimes if there are others like me out there—other people with their own versions of the house at the end of North Cedar. Haunted places that don't exist, not in this version of reality, anyway, but maybe in some other place and time. In some other world, remembered only by a few. There's gotta be, right? There were a shitload of doors in that weird forest and all of those trees, twisted and oddly human? Had those all been people once, like Jackie? When I say it out loud, it sounds crazy as fuck, totally impossible. If thousands of people remember Mandela dying, however, even though that never happened, then why not this?

But then I think this is probably all just a bunch of bullshit—a terrible, half-remembered nightmare I concocted to make sense of losing two friends. Probably, Jackie and Scooter did get hit by a train while drunk. Maybe the Coyotes picked over their bodies.

Maybe.

Some part of me hopes so, because the other alternative is too fuckin' scary to get my head around—and probably not for the reason you're thinking. Sure, what happened was traumatizing as shit, that goes without saying, but what I'm really worried about is that someday down the road he might come back for me.

34

'Cause, here's the thing, it seems that once the Mandela Effect takes root in the collective hive-mind of humanity, more and more people begin to remember. It's like catching a mental cold—a virus passed on through belief, imagination, and memory. And the more people who remember, who believe, the more real it becomes. And maybe that's not such a big deal with little things—like Shazam or Curious George's tail—but what about the monster that lived in the house at the end of North Cedar Street? Will that collective belief spawn more houses and more windows for Mr. Flysuit to gaze through?

And if it does, how long before someone slips up and lets him through for good? How long before he finds a way to let himself into my home? Or into yours?

LAST BUS TO BROOKLYN

MELISSA KOONS

It's hard to accept the evil in this world. People choose to ignore the horror that occurs on their own streets, preferring to turn a blind eye rather than to admit the depth of darkness that can consume a person's soul. I've worked too long in this profession to deny it any more. I've seen the horrors one person is capable of committing when they unleash the monster within. I wasn't prepared to see that kind of darkness on my first case. It shocked me, disturbed me, and chilled me to my core—just like it would anyone. Now, after twenty years of it, I barely let out a shudder. That kind of constant exposure to the darkness changes a man. He either hardens to the world in order to keep going, or he succumbs to it. I've seen one too many good detectives fold at the barrel-end of their own service weapon. That's why I choose to work alone, now. Not everyone can harden themselves to this work, but I can.

Many men in my line of work keep themselves separate from the streets they have to clean, but not me. I like to swim among the sea of vagabonds I bring to justice. I live among

36

them, walk beside them, and watch them from the windows of an old bus while it ambles by. I take the same bus every night— the last of the line, so if I miss it, I am shit out of luck. Every night it's the same familiar crew of characters who sit on board the half-full, silent bus as it meanders through the dark and vacant streets. The florescent lights hum while we all stare out the windows and ignore each other's existence; anyone out past 1:30 in the morning in Brooklyn was not someone you wanted to make small talk with.

The bus lurches to a stop and I watch from my seat in the back as she gets on. She is the prettiest girl I've ever seen, and I know she doesn't belong on this bus. Night after night she gets on this bus, gives me a slight smile, and takes a seat a few rows up. I often stare at her the rest of my trip, wondering what a girl like that was going through to be on a bus like this.

When I first saw her, I was concerned. I thought maybe she had lost her way or her bachelorette party had deserted her, so I kept an eye on her. I keep an eye on everyone, but especially on her. She seemed a little shaken—like she knew she was on the wrong bus going nowhere, but didn't know what else to do. The old stripper heading to work for the morning shift gave her a reassuring smile, and the girl's shoulders slumped with ease. That's when I knew she chose to be on the wrong bus for a reason. Night after night, it became a routine. She would get on at the same stop, ride for about five miles, and then get off. The other passengers didn't hassle her, threaten her, or scare her. They accepted her as one of their late-night own—which was worse.

She didn't start smiling at me until I ran into her at the precinct. She had been caught giving a hand job to some loser in a back parking lot for fifty bucks. I wasn't the officer on the case—I don't work those kinds of cases—so I wasn't sure if she would recognize me the next time she climbed onto our bus. Like I said, we all had an unspoken agreement to let each other be. It seems she did recognize me, though. The night after her release, she climbed up those steps and met my observing gaze with a small smile. That was months ago. We never speak a word to each other, just that one tilt of her lips in acknowledgement, and that is it.

Tonight, though, she doesn't give me that smile. Her hands are wrapped around her and she climbs up the stairs with unsteady footing. Her eyes scan all the seats and finally land on me. I expect the smile, but she doesn't give one. Instead, she lets out a shaky breath and stumbles her way toward me with a distinct purpose. Her heavy eye make-up is smeared down her cheeks—from rain or tears, I'm not sure. One of her outrageous heels is broken, explaining her uneven steps, but causing me to question why it had broken in the first place. She takes the seat directly in front of me, sliding in so that she is sitting sideways. She looks up at me pitifully, pleadingly, yet doesn't say a word.

The bus rolls up to my stop and I get off. I'm not surprised to hear her broken heels clopping after me as I descend the stairs to the street. I wait for her to come and stand beside me, but she doesn't. She stops a few steps back, but I can still feel her watching me. The bus lets out a hiss as the driver closes the door and it lurches forward, continuing on its unsavory route. I glance over my shoulder and she's still standing there, waiting for me. Her hair is damp and her curls have fallen out, it hangs in dreary waves around her heart-shaped face, making her look more like a soaked mouse than a young woman. There's the budding of a deep bruise blooming on her cheek, and her eyes are wide and frightened. I tilt my head in the direction of the precinct and start on my way. I listen to her footsteps as she follows me from her safe distance; she still doesn't speak, and I'm not about to start up any conversation.

She follows silently, three steps behind me all the way to the precinct. I glance back at her only once, the sound of her uneven heels clacking behind me lets me know she is still there. Pulling open the door, the precinct is bustling—as it always is regardless of the time. I weave between officers hustling paper work and dodge criminals begging for their phone calls as they are escorted to their holding cells. I nod to my colleagues as they pass by, tipping my hat to Johnny as he answers another call. Heaving a sigh, I take my seat at my desk and remove my hat, tossing it to the side. I look up into her teary eyes as she makes her way uncertainly through the chaos towards me. I gesture toward the chair in front of my desk, hoping she will sit down and take off those stupid shoes.

Hesitantly, she pulls out the chair just enough for her slight frame to slide into it. She twists her hands in her torn, sodden jacket and her eyes dart around the office. She nibbles on her lower lip, and bounces her knee in an anxious silence.

I lean back in my chair, folding my hands in my lap, and wait for her to say something—anything. Not for the first time, I imagine what her sweet voice might sound like. Eventually, her attention lands back on me and she opens her mouth for a brief moment, before thinking twice and closing it again. Frustrated that she has robbed me momentarily of the opportunity to finally hear her story, I decide to give her a break as fresh tears stream down her cheeks, drawing the black smears of her make-up further down the pale curves of her face.

"Detective," Johnny says, coming up to my desk. His face is somber as he drops a familiarly thick file on my desk. "He's back."

I stare at the file on my desk, worn around the edges from years of handling. I hoped I would never see this file pulled out again. It may be my job to work homicide cases, but this one I want to shove into a drawer and forget about. "How long ago?" I ask, lifting the cover of the folder to gander at the crime scene photos I've seen a hundred times. I hear a sharp intake of breath and look up into her wide, frightened eyes as she stares at the disturbed scenes. I close the file to shield her from any more upsetting images.

"About two hours ago. The scene has been taped off and they're waiting for you." Johnny says.

I purse my lips, still gazing at the sunken beauty across from me. "I'll meet you at the car." I tell Johnny.

Johnny nods and walks away, off to pull the car around front.

Standing, I grab my hat and set it on my head while I make my way toward the door. I pause briefly beside her on my way out, and she looks up at me with such dread that I have to swallow a lump in my throat. "It's best if you stay here. You can wait for me to get back, otherwise someone else will be capable of helping you with whatever you need." I say to her.

She doesn't move or make any acknowledgement as to what I said, she simply continues to gaze up at me like a lost kitten.

Not sure what to make of her, I give her a nod and leave, regretting every step I take away from her.

"It's his typical M.O." Johnny says, briefing me as we speed toward the scene. There are few cars on the road, but the flashing red light is still turned on to ensure no one slows us down.

"Victim?" I ask, pulling out a smoke and cracking the window. The car hits another bump and my match slips against the box, not getting enough friction to ignite. I give

Johnny a sidelong glance and he just clears his throat, slowing down a little as we hit the next dip in the road.

"A girl—about twenty. She's only got one prior, but it's definitely his work." Johnny says confidently.

I strike my match and inhale deeply as I light the tip of my cigarette, taking the smoke deep into my lungs. "How can you be so sure?" I had to make sure it was him. Not just any case was allowed in that file. Maybe this one was just a coincidence—or a copycat even.

Johnny shakes his head and slows to a stop just outside an alley behind a familiar Chinese restaurant on the East side of town. Both ends of the alley were taped off with a bright yellow barrier and flashing police lights danced across the brick walls. "It's him. He did her body just like all the others." He says, climbing out of the car.

I take another puff and open my door. The alley was narrow, only wide enough to fit a dumpster and the truck that picks it up. I follow behind Johnny as he leads the way through the other blue coats and the coroner filling out paper work. I glance at the young man in a white apron talking to one of the officers, giving his statement no doubt. He must have been the poor soul who found her.

Johnny stops a little ways off and gestures toward the ground. A camera flashes and he squints at the brightness as forensics does their best to capture the scene exactly as they found it.

I crouch down beside her and can't help the exasperated puff of air that escapes my lips. I put my cigarette out in a little puddle of rainwater beside my shoes and try to rub the weariness from my face with both hands. I take a deep breath in and let it out slowly, letting my hands drop to rest on my bent knees. I want to tell Johnny he was wrong; I want to tell him this was just a deal gone badly and it wasn't our guy, but I can't. There is no denying the oh-so-familiar style that belongs only to him. I tilt my head and look at the body from every angle I can without moving from my spot.

She was dead before he flung her down on the wet pavement. Her body lay crumpled on the ground, one leg bent under her at an awkward angle with her torso twisted in an unnatural position that only could have happened from being dropped that way. Her cheek is bruised and slightly cut from the impact where it had hit the tiny rocks on the street; he threw her down with a lot of force to cause that kind of injury. The red marks around her neck show the tell-tale signs of strangulation, and the bloody, broken fingernails prove that she fought back. "Well honey, you tried to get away, but it just didn't work out." I mutter to myself, taking in her torn jacket and broken heel. I'll never understand why women wear those stupid things. They're a death trap.

I take a pen out of my coat pocket and used the tip to lift a corner of her sodden jacket. "Shit." I cover my face with my hand and groan. "Where are they?" I ask, lifting my head to look at Johnny.

His face went white and he shifts his feet, looking down at the pavement before tilting his head. He clears his throat and glances over at the two, neat piles a few feet from her head. "They, uh, they're right over there. He left a new list, too." He says, his voice as shaky as his legs.

I let her jacket fall back down and stand up, craning my neck to peer over her limp curls. "Shit." I curse again. If those two piles, so perfectly arranged, hadn't been there I could have said this was a mugging, a crime of passion, anything else but him. But no, there they were—complete with his list—his signature calling card. I walk toward the piles and size them up. One pile consisted of neatly folded women's clothing. A light pink sweater, a brown plaid skirt, a pair of brown stockings, and a pair of brown, sensible, flat-heeled shoes. Classy. The list was pinned to the sweater on the top of the pile with a pair of women's glasses resting beside it. "Let's see what he chose for you," I say, crouching down. I glance over at the other pile and suppress a shiver.

"Para legal, librarian, secretary, assistant, filing clerk— they're all nice office jobs he picked." Johnny says, gesturing toward the list.

I nod my head and look back at her body. My eyes slide over the young woman and I try to imagine her out of those outrageous heels, that sodden jacket and into this classic ensemble he chose for her. I try to picture her without the heavy black eye-makeup running down her lifeless cheeks and with a smile on her lips. I can see what he must have saw. She would have been well suited for office work.

Now, it doesn't really matter. She'd stain the sweater red if she tried to put it on. My eyes flick over to the second pile. It was just as neatly stacked as the first, but far more upsetting in its contents. He had layered the small intestine on the ground first, followed by the large, then her lungs, her stomach, her liver, and then her heart. They stacked so perfectly—just like a pile of folded clothes. It was almost as if they were accessories he left for her to pick and choose from, like jewelry or a pair of women's glasses.

"Why does he do it that way?" Johnny asks, his voice soft so the others milling about the scene won't hear him.

I stand up and return to my spot beside him. I light up another cigarette and take a long drag. I stare at the pile of organs, rubbing the butt of my cigarette across my lips. I see Johnny turn toward the car out of the corner of my eye and realize he had been waiting for my reply. "It's so he can weigh and measure them."

Johnny stops and looks at me, his young face twisted in confusion. "Measure them for what?" He asks.

I inhale deeply and feel the smoke burn my throat and lungs in an almost unbearable discomfort that makes me feel alive. I turn away from her and head back to the car, Johnny following behind me. I slide into the front seat and flick the ash from my cigarette before answering.

"For their final judgement."

It's raining again, but it doesn't bother me. I stand outside the precinct, my hat low over my eyes as I smoke another cigarette. Whenever we get a new case file on him, one smoke doesn't cut it. Whatever resolution I have to quit goes out the window and I find myself going through a pack a night. Oh well. It hasn't killed me yet. The rain drizzles around me, the molding on the building providing a small lip that keeps me dry. Johnny had parked the car and gone inside ages ago, which is why I knew it was only a matter of time before she came to find me. I took another drag and shook my head. I felt her standing beside me rather than hear her this time, the noise from inside drowning out the click of her broken heels.

"Anubis," I say even though she didn't ask. "That's what we call him. He's been performing his last rites on victims for fifteen years." I'm met with silence so I glance over at her and let out a breath of smoke.

She shakes her head and tears drip from her chin and fall with the rain. "Why?" She mouths soundlessly.

Guiltily, I look away from her. I wish I had an answer that would make her feel better—but I don't.

"Wasted potential." I sniff, rubbing my nose which is cold from the rain. We stand in silence after that, watching my cigarette burn down in the early morning darkness.

"Detective, the body was identified," Johnny pokes his head out of the front doors, grabbing my attention.

44

"Name?" I ask. Taking a long, deep drag.

He flips open the file in his hands and reminds himself of the victim's identity. "Her name is Anna Fields."

I give a nod and he heads back into the precinct. I blow the smoke out slowly, pursing my lips and making a smoke ring that dissolves in the wet air. I snuff out my cigarette on the side of the building and drop the butt onto the pavement. I look up at her standing frigid on the front steps waiting for me. "Alright Anna, let's go back inside," I say and open the door.

The picture becomes clearer as I flip through the file. I look up at her where she sits across from me at my desk. Age: 23; hair color: dark brown; eye color: dark brown; last known residence: Queens, NY. She ran away at fifteen. She lived with her older, half-sister until she was nineteen, then her sister kicked her out so her boyfriend could move in, instead. That's when Anna came to Brooklyn. She had only a few hundred dollars to her name—which was enough to find a room to rent but not much else.

Anna shifts uncomfortably in her chair. She wraps her coat tighter around her and pulls her knees up to her chest, curling into a ball on the wooden seat.

"Why did you come to Brooklyn, Anna?" I ask her, my voice low and my nose still buried in her file.

She shrugs and peeks at me over her knees. "Where else was I going to go?" Her voice is soft and hesitant—like a water soaked mouse addressing the cat who saved it.

"You could have gone anywhere from Queens." I sigh, flipping the page.

"With what? I had no money, no family, and no connections. A girl I met on the streets when I was fifteen said she was heading here because there were jobs. That's all I had to go on, and I had just enough for a bus ticket."

I nod my head. "That must have been the first night you were here."

Her brow furrows and she lets her feet slide off the edge of the chair and fall to the floor. "When?" she asked.

"The first time I saw you on that bus headed nowhere. You looked so unsure—like you didn't belong. You didn't belong on that bus."

Her eyes narrow and her glare is fierce. "You have been watching me since then?"

I nod my head once.

"Do you know how creepy that is?" She spits.

I lift my eyes and fix her with my gaze for the first time since getting her file. "You always smiled back. No one on that bus ever acknowledges anyone."

Shaking her head she scoffs and lets out a harsh laugh. "I smiled because some creepy old guy was always watching me when I boarded an empty bus. If that nice stripper lady was riding, I always sat near her because she eased the tension."

I frown and let the file close. "That's why you sat by her?"

Anna scoffs. "Hell yeah. You freaked me out—for good reason. That first time I boarded the bus it was just the two of you, and you didn't blink. You just stared at me. When she smiled at me, I felt better because she obviously rode the bus with you frequently and she was okay."

I shake my head. No. That couldn't be right. She knew me. She knew I would protect her. She must have sensed that I would save her from a life of destitute. She could be so much more than what she was settling for. I saw the look between her and the old stripper, I knew she thought that was going to be her ticket to a comfortable life. She smiled at me because she wanted me to save her. So I did. "What about when you got arrested?"

She blows air out between her lips. "What? That time I was giving my boyfriend a hand job in a parking lot?"

I shake my head. "He paid you for it. You don't need to lie to me, I saw the case file." When I pulled that case file I knew it was her first step down a path to nowhere. She'd be riding that bus for the rest of her days if someone didn't intervene.

Anna tossed her head back and gave a loud, humorless laugh. "That wasn't payment for the hand job. That was rent money. I covered for him the previous month and he was paying me back. You cops are all alike. You see a poor couple in a car late at night and assume I'm turning tricks."

"You do work at a bar off Myrtle Avenue."

"So what, I'm automatically a hooker for that?" She bites.

I shake my head and take a deep breath in. "No, but we watch that area closely. We've caught several women prostituting near there." I defend.

"You sound just like that square officer who interrogated me. No, I'm not a whore. It was just bad timing." She sneers.

I glance at her, letting my eyes go up and down her figure—taking in her choice of clothing and make-up, all of which was now torn, soaking wet, and running down her cheeks. "Then why do you dress like that? That skirt is a little too short, those heels a little too tall, and you've got an awful lot of make-up on for just working at a bar."

Anna sneered and pulled her skirt down her thigh a little more. "It's called making tips. Besides, I wasn't just working tonight. A few girl friends and I went out after my shift to celebrate; one of them got engaged. Didn't you ever go out

47

when you were younger? Were you ever younger? You look like you've been fifty for the last ten years, old man."

I ignore her quip about my age—I do feel like I've been fifty for the last ten years, but in my line of work the stress will do that to you. I'm not sure why she's lying to me, she has no reason to lie to me now. I know she was brought in on charges of prostitution. I flip open the file again and read her arrest record.

"Yeah, read it again sweetheart. Charges for prostitution were dismissed. We still had to deal with the whole public lewdness thing, but that was it." She squares her shoulders and tightens her jaw.

I review the case and she is right. It had been updated after I initially skimmed it. Still, she knew I was a detective. She smiled at me because she recognized me. I know she did. That's how she asked me to help her; she knew I could.

"So you were just a waitress?" I ask her.

She nods and purses her lips. "Yup. I *was* just a waitress." A tear slips down her cheek and she juts out her jaw as she tries to hold the rest back. "I don't get it. Why? Why did *Anubis* do this?" She asks, shaking her head.

A lump forms in my throat and I drum my fingers on the desk, itching for a smoke. My voice is steady when I answer her. I keep it void of emotion—hollow, factual. "Anubis selects his victims based on those he believes have wasted their potential."

She sits silently, her eyes flicking around the room as her mind works to process my simple answer. Her lips part, opening and closing without words. "I just smiled." She whimpers.

My eyebrows drew together in confusion. Of course she smiled. That's how I knew. "What do you mean you 'just smiled'?"

Anna's eyes lock onto mine and the tears flow hot and heavy down her face. Her chest rises with each breath she draws in and her gazes burns me. "I only smiled. That was my crime. I smiled to avoid an awkward situation. Wasted potential? What the fuck does *Anubis* know? I was making my rent. I was making enough tips to buy food. My boyfriend and I had problems, but we were working through them. I had more than I ever had in my life. I had enough that I could go out with my friends for a night and not worry about eating the next day or where I was going to be staying. *Wasted?*"

Standing up she leans over the desk until her nose almost touches mine. "WASTED? I wasted nothing! I fought! I was building myself up the best that I could. I didn't have any breaks. I didn't finish high school, I had no other education. That list? That fucking list of jobs? That's what would have been filling my potential?" She pauses and shakes her head. She straightens and pulls on her hair, her eyes closing at what should have been a comforting sting.

"My job isn't my potential. Riding the last bus to Brooklyn wasn't my potential. I am so much more than those things. They do not define me and what I am capable of; neither does my short skirt, my too tall heels, or my heavy eye make-up. Potential takes time, and mine was stolen from me." She screams. Her voice quivers with agony and pain.

My nails dig into the wood of the desk. I need a cigarette. Pushing myself away from the desk I bolt for the door. The crisp air hits my face like tiny needles. My hands shake as I try to light the cigarette in my mouth. It takes me three tries to get my match to strike.

She is right. She deserved more than that. She deserved to be more than a file on my desk, never to be solved. How could I have been so wrong? She wanted my help, didn't she? That's why she smiled. The dawn lights the sky and its soft rays feel like harsh judgement on my skin.

"Hey detective, end of your shift?" Henderson asks, walking up the steps to start his day.

I give him a courteous nod as he passes. "Not yet, but soon." I inhale the nicotine deeply into my lungs and hold it there until it burns. The cigarette burns down too quickly and I find myself without distraction. I walk through the precinct slowly, dreading seeing her at my desk again—but when I reach my post she's gone. Her file lays open where I left it, the pictures from the crime scene decorating the surface. The stack of secretarial clothing, her organs, the list. The pictures are silent, but the images are not.

Wasted potential. She could have been so much more. She should have been so much more. A smile. Her crime was a smile. A smile begging for help. A smile begging for more—at least, that's what I had thought. Was I really that wrong? I close the folder and add it to the rest that belong to him. She will never get the closure she deserves. Neither of us will. I grab my hat and head back out into the cold, morning light.

"Have a good night, Johnny. Say 'hi' to the wife and kids for me," I tell him as we pass each other on our way out.

He gives me a nod and carries on his way, heading toward the garage for the car.

I prefer to take the bus. I like to swim among the sea of vagabonds I bring to justice. I live among them, walk beside them, and watch them from the windows of an old bus while it ambles by. I take the same bus every morning, and every morning it's the same familiar crew of characters who sit on board the half-full, silent bus. I climb the steps, my eyes scanning all the familiar faces.

"Rough night?" the middle-aged stripper asks me, just getting off her shift, as well.

I give the stripper a tight-lipped smile and look away. "You could say that," I mutter. I hear a familiar *clop* down the aisle and turn to see Anna walk toward me. She doesn't smile at me this time. She doesn't smile at me ever again. She sits down beside me and looks at the stripper who had offered her comfort her first night, and every night up until her last.

"How are the kids?" I ask, swallowing the lump in my throat.

The stripper beams at me and adjusts her purse on her lap. "They're good! Thanks for askin'. My sister should be droppin' them off at school right about now on her way to work. That'll give me just enough time to get some sleep before I pick them up and we go to the park. After all the rain last night, I hope it will be a sunny day," she rambles.

I don't care to listen. I turn away, gazing out the window as she continues to prattle on, avoiding the eyes I feel on my back. The bus comes to a halt and she stops talking, silence descending upon the crowded bus once more. After a minute, no one gets on. The bus driver looks down the sidewalk, checking to see if his regular was running down the block just a few minutes late. The streets and sidewalks were empty, so the driver shrugs and closes the door, continuing his route.

"Do you remember that young girl who used to get on at that stop?" the stripper asks, pulling my attention back to her.

I stiffen, my eyes gliding over that very girl who is seated beside me. "I recall a young woman once or twice. What of it?"

The stripper keeps her eyes on the door, not looking my way and lets out a sigh. "I haven't seen her. She usually gets on at that stop. I hope she's okay."

"I'm sure she's fine," I say through pressed lips and a forced smile.

The stripper relaxes a little and smiles back at me. "You're probably right. It's the mother in me, I can't help but to worry."

A tear falls down Anna's cheek but she remains silent. They all do.

I tap my fingers on my knee, scratching at the fabric of my slacks. I want to light up, but not here.

"I mean," she continues despite my lack of attention, "it's hard not to notice that she's missing. Maybe she's ill," the stripper suggests.

Clearing my throat, I turn and address the woman, but I focus left of her face, my eyes staring into Anna's. "What makes you say that?"

The stripper laughs and clutches her purse a little tighter, avoiding my eyes as she continues to watch the door. "Well dear, you and I are the only ones who ride this bus regularly. It's noticeable when someone gets on, or off."

One by one, I look at all the faces surrounding me. They each occupy a seat. They all sit silently. Distracted, they gaze out of windows or down at their hands. As I focus on each person, they turn and their eyes lock on to mine. A surge of familiarity rushes through me with each pair. He fought. He didn't. She screamed. He cried. She gasped. He yelled. She smiled.

"Were they all wasting their potential, too?" Anna asks, gazing around at the company she had never seen before last night, but all of whom rode this bus.

The man in his thirties three rows up, window seat: he fought. His folder held three accounts of assault and battery charges. He could have been an athlete. He had had a scholarship for boxing at a state university. He turned it down, but kept fighting on the side in illegal rings.

"Maybe she just moved on. So many of them do, they never seem to ride this bus for very long. Just you and me," the stripper rambles. Her knuckles are white as they clutch her bag and her jaw is tight as she watches the door.

The middle-aged man the row behind and adjacent to me, leaning against the wall of the bus: he didn't fight. The market shifted and he lost all his stock. He lost his house, his wife, his job. He had an advanced degree, but he didn't pick himself back up. He started conning people, giving them bad tips for a large fee; cashing out before they lost what little they had.

The bus slows to a stop and the stripper lets out a soft sigh. "Well, this is me. See you tomorrow," she rushes off the bus with a wave over her shoulder.

The woman in her late twenties the seat in front of me: she screamed. She was brought in on charges of disturbing the peace and domestic abuse, and she had two prior accounts of hitting a minor, as well. She had screamed at her husband, waking up the neighbors, and was throwing things at him when the police arrived on scene. She gave him a black eye and broke two of his ribs because he wasn't home on time. He couldn't lift a hand to defend himself, the last time he had tried she claimed abuse and he spent thirty days in lock down.

I lean back in my seat and watch the stripper walk away until the bus pulls out and resumes its route.

"How long are you going to let her live?" Anna asks me.

I look around at all the other souls and let out a deep breath. He cried. She gasped. He yelled. She smiled. My nails pick at a loose thread in the weave of my pants and I swallow, trying to push down the lump in my throat. "She's fulfilling her potential. She's good to her kids." I tell her.

She falls silent again until the bus gets to my stop.

The teenage boy near the driver: he cried. He ran away from home and started dealing drugs on the street. He targeted kids like him, and dealt near schools. He took what he dealt and would sit on the bus sobbing until his high wore off. He lost half his teeth and the color in his face until the drugs made his skin thin and gray.

I exit and I hear the clicking of her broken heels follow me. I climb up the flights of stairs to my dingy apartment, the rustle of their clothing behind me.

The middle-aged woman who dyed her hair: she gasped. She stepped off the curb too early in front of a cab. It only ran over her foot, but she gasped in pain and the settlement was hefty. Once the money ran out, she tried the same con again but was arrested for fraud: on three separate occasions.

I've seen the horrors one person is capable of committing when they unleash the monster within. I've worked too long in this profession to deny it any more. That kind of constant exposure to the darkness changes a man. He either hardens to the world in order to keep going, or he succumbs to it.

The man in his twenties, not much older than Anna: he yelled. He screamed at the bus driver for being late to his stop. He yelled at women walking down the street. He yelled at anyone who disagreed with him, or told him that he was wrong. He had a record of harassment—both verbal and physical—that was two pages long, yet he never seemed to learn. He ruined a promising law career and later a career in marketing.

I pull my curtains tight, shutting out the sun. Crawling into bed, I can hear their breathing filling the silent room. They file in and take their posts in the tiny space. I couldn't have been wrong about all of them. They wasted their potential, I saw it night in and night out on that bus.

Anna takes her spot at the foot of my bed. I close my eyes, blocking them out. I was right to help them. They needed my help and I gave it to them. No longer were they fighting, crying, yelling, or screaming.

"You have been weighed," Anna whispers in my ear. The weight of her hovers over me.

I shudder. No longer were they smiling.

"You have been measured," her non-existent breath tickles my ear.

I surrendered to the darkness that lurks within every man. I had no choice, I've seen one too many good detectives fold at the barrel-end of their own service weapon—that wasn't going to be me.

"You have been judged," she hisses.

I like to swim among the sea of vagabonds I bring to justice. I am just like them. Potential wasted, chasing an illusion that will never be caught even as it stares me in the face.

"Your time will come, and when it does you will burn. We can wait, Anubis, we have no other potential left to fulfill." She crawls back to her spot at the edge of my bed.

She tells me nothing I haven't heard before. Seventeen times, in fact. I open my eyes and look at them all. Seventeen lives wasted. Seventeen who could have been so much more. Seventeen who got on the wrong bus to Brooklyn. The last bus to anywhere.

"I know," I whisper to the empty room.

PENNED IN GALL

EMILY GODHAND

Kayla wasn't much for parties, but when the prettiest, smartest, kindest woman at your college invited you to her family's mountain home, how could you turn her down? I mean, sure, the invitation had technically been addressed to 'K', so it could have been her roommate Kathryn. But no one ever invited Kayla to parties. This was her chance to make friends. To her credit, she did tell her roommate, but the art major felt ill and gave her blessing for Kayla to go in her stead. That, and, her roommate knew how much Kayla admired Jaiden. Everyone knew that.

Except Jaiden, it seemed.

From a distance, the mountain home blended naturally into the Rockies with its wooden walls and stone decor. Kayla parked on the shoulder of the winding driveway and walked up to the mansion. She froze on the staircase ascending to the porch of the first floor. A triangular, second-story, balcony sat atop the two angled rooms that made up the first story. A holy trinity.

Jaiden stood on the balcony by herself. Kayla recognized her instantly from her cropped, black hair; brilliant, green eyes; and unflappable confidence to wear a string bikini at the start of the party. Kayla shifted her backpack onto her shoulder and wondered when she should change into her swimsuit. Jaiden stared ahead over the mountain, lost in thought. She bit her wine-colored lip and narrowed her eyes at something. The sun was behind the house. It couldn't have been the sunset. Maybe she was worried about the lighting for the party?

Someone bumped into Kayla's shoulder on the way up the broad stairs. She stumbled and picked herself up. Maybe this wasn't such a good idea. But Denver was 90 minutes behind her and she'd just watch Netflix with Kathryn again, anyway.

She looked up at the balcony again, but Jaiden was gone.

Inside, the guests were quieter than she expected. Most of them had their faces stuffed with food from the buffet like chipmunks before winter, and they let the overwhelming music and their attempt at dance moves do the talking for them. She spotted the engineering students playing Jenga in the corner and the English majors had started a game of Scrabble that seemed to be getting out of hand over whether "theatre" was an acceptable spelling. Two pre-med students appeared to have been studying anatomy in the bathroom together as they giggled and adjusted their clothing as they left.

Kayla wasn't sure where a communications major who found it hard to speak to people belonged at this party. If she belonged at all. She was a five-foot nothing pear-shaped bundle of anxiety and felt she was going to be sick. Everyone else's make-up was perfect, and she felt like a sixth grader who discovered the dollar store. She just wanted a chance to get to know Jaiden and what her life was like, what the girl who seemed to have everything wanted out of life. But she had enough friends, she didn't need her. Kayla didn't want to leave, though. Maybe this would make a good story for the school paper.

She grabbed a cold beer out of the ice bucket by the buffet table and decided to test her luck with the English majors. She introduced herself, but her soft voice was drowned out by laughter as the theater majors joined the discussion. She chugged the beer down and grabbed another one when a philosophy major introduced himself. As a philosophy major. He invited her to a 'civil debate' and wasn't getting the message she wasn't interested when she kept drinking and nodding instead of answering.

By Kayla's fourth beer, Jaiden had stepped in to settle the matter of Scrabble, calling them all nerds, and Kayla could barely contain her excitement. At some point, Jaiden had jumped into the pool and was now dripping water all over the hardwood floors. She casually dried her hair while chastising the underclassmen. Jaiden turned to Kayla next. Kayla knew she was speaking, something about their classes, but she didn't hear a word. She was transfixed on the tattoo of the Eye of Providence over Jaiden's heart. She didn't want to stare at her breasts, but they were beautiful, too, and the tattoo seemed to have glitter on it.

Kayla put on a dumbfounded smile and screamed internally. She took a sip of beer to buy herself time to come up with words that weren't creepy and promptly choked on the foam. It spilled out of the bottle and down the front of her shirt.

Everyone saw. Jaiden saw. And was now staring at her breasts for an entirely different reason.

Kayla held still, wide-eyed as a deer, as the bottle foamed everywhere. Jaiden grinned and handed her towel to her.

"I'm s-so sorry," stammered Kayla as wiped up the mess. She frowned at how wet her white shirt was and covered herself with the crumbled towel. It smelled like Jaiden; like sunshine and whisky and late-night cigarettes. The philosophy major was still talking in the background.

Jaiden shook her head and laughed it off. "It happens. Gives you a chance to change into your swimsuit, right?", she said. Kayla imagined she winked. Did she imagine it? No, she winked. Did she want to see her in her swimsuit or—?

No, she told herself, *she's just being polite because this is a pool party. Take the save you awkward pigeon.*

Kayla excused herself to the bathroom. The pre-meds had advanced to their residency in the downstairs bathroom, so she tiptoed to the one upstairs. She changed, self-conscious of her one-piece suit when everyone else boasted cute bikini tops. What a first impression to make: drunk and half-naked and already made a fool of herself. Oh well, at least that made her no different than everyone else at college parties, right?

She crept down the hall to the bedroom and the designated coat-bed. She set her things down and pulled out her phone. Okay, so maybe everyone else was downstairs socializing and here she was checking if there was a signal to text Katie. Nothing. She bet the Wi-Fi password was downstairs, too.

No, wait, there was a computer desk littered with empty glasses. Yes, she, too, had avoided the walk of shame of taking the various cups to the kitchen. Kayla tried to check one of the drawers and found it stuck. She wiggled with it until it finally opened but knocked one of the glasses down. Kayla cursed, and winced as it shattered on the floor.

"Hello? Is anyone there?" whispered a quiet voice from the closet.

Kayla gingerly picked up the pieces of glass and hissed as a sharp edge sliced her finger. She needed to hurry before someone discovered her mistake. One glass missing wouldn't matter, right?

"Please, help me. I won't let me out," whispered the voice again. It came distinctly from the closet this time. Kayla glanced up and sucked on her bleeding finger. Did someone play a prank? She opened the door. The voice repeated its pleas, louder. Kayla turned on the single overhead light with a pull of the string. Pressed pants and silk blouses filled the closet. She ran her uninjured hand over the paneling and knocked until she heard a hollow echo.

Hidden within the closet was a secret door to a room that should not have existed. Kayla had passed the bathroom on the way to the bedroom, so there was no room for a 13x13 hidden closet in the same space. Physics wouldn't allow it. Empty bookshelves lined the walls, about a shoulder's width wide and shoulder's height tall. A stone pedestal in the middle held a glass dome with a small, glowing, pink bubble that threw itself against its prison like a trapped firefly.

"Let me out!" it cried in its tiny voice. "Let me out, I'm going to kill us all."

Had she hit her head? Kayla crawled into the room and approached the little bubble.

"Please, you cannot trust me," pleaded the bubble ghost. Something about the voice reminded her of Jaiden's.

"You're not making the best case for your freedom," said Kayla. Maybe someone had slipped something into her drink? She touched the glass and felt a thrum against her hand. It wasn't a physical barrier at all and gave under pressure. Written into the side was a sigil, like a sharp E in a triangle. A lightning strike through an L. She traced her finger over the sigil, starting at the bottom and going up, down, right—

"Thank you," whispered the ghost. The barrier disappeared. Crap. She didn't know that would happen. The ground rumbled.

"Let me in," commanded the ghost. Kayla shook her head. Another rumble and she lost her footing. The ghost darted into Kayla's chest, and the lights went out as her head struck the pedestal.

Everything felt wrong when Kayla woke up at noon. At least that's what her broken phone said. Kayla crawled through the sticky, coffee-grounds of her own headwound out of the impossible closet. The coats and backpacks were still on the bed. Out the window, a starless, moonless night sky pressed itself onto the house. Another shimmering barrier blocked the door and locked her in.

"Actually, it's to keep them out," said the ghost's voice.

Kayla grabbed her chest, where she felt a warmth in her core, and gasped. "Why the hell are you inside me?"

"You didn't exactly say no, and I needed somewhere to hide."

"That doesn't mean 'yes'!" Kayla took a deep breath, half expecting the ghost to be exhaled. If this were a drunken dream, might as well ride it out. "Who are you?"

"I'm Jaiden. Who are you?"

"Jaiden is downstairs. We met already."

"That's not me. I think I'd have remembered you."

"Oh, great, I didn't make enough of an impression to be missed," said Kayla. "I'm just going to call you Jade instead."

"So, I can stay?"

"Fine, whatever."

She held her head in her hands and rocked on the edge of the bed. Her phone rang, and she flinched. She couldn't make out the text on the screen no matter how much she blinked.

"Don't answer that," whispered Jade.

Kayla hushed her and answered the phone. "H-Hello?"

"I didn't invite you to this party," said Jaiden's voice. Her voice was eerily calm. Curious even. "What made you want to come anyway?"

"You gotta help me. I don't know what's going on. I hit my head badly. Please, I'm upstairs—"

"Oh, now you found a tongue?"

Kayla bit hers and sniffled. "Whatever. Winter Park is nearby. I think I need an ambulance. I'm hearing voices and—"

"Did you ever wonder why God doesn't answer your prayers?" asked Jaiden.

Kayla shook her head and pushed herself to her feet. Her shoes dragged across the floor as she made her way to the shimmering barrier blocking the door.

"Because he wasn't the one listening, K."

Call ended.

"What is that supposed to mean?" whispered Kayla. She hit the emergency call button on the phone. No signal.

"You really shouldn't talk to me," said Jade. "I can get inside your head."

Kayla pressed on the glimmering barrier, trying to remember what the sigil in the closet looked like. Left, right, left, right...

The barrier seemed to shimmer even more.

"I wouldn't do that if I were you", said Jade. "That way it says 'Banish', but more accurately it means 'contain'."

"How do you even know that?"

"I'm the one that put it there," said the voice inside her. "I locked myself away once I realized what I was doing.

62

Everyone was invited for a reason, but you weren't supposed to be here. I wanted to protect you—"

"Shut up and let me think," said Kayla. She held her throbbing head and felt her hand sticky and wet. Crap. At least the bleeding had stopped. How to erase it? She drew the sigil again, in reverse this time. Up, down, left...

The barrier shimmered and shattered into pieces that evaporated into the ether. One more layer left. Kayla drew the shape again, and they were free.

Now, most houses are built similarly, in that the space they occupy keeps the same dimensions and the rooms stay in the same locations. Maybe it was the massive head trauma, the drink, or all a dream, but this house in particular had the damned temerity to change it up on Kayla. Her feet should have been standing in the hallway, next to the bathroom. She should see a line of bedrooms. At the end of the hall, there should have been two staircases: one going up to the third story master, and one going down to the living room and the party guests. She should've easily put one foot in front of the other and called out over the railing, and someone would have screamed, and someone else would drive her to the hospital where they'd chide her on the evils of drinking and claim it was all one vivid nightmare she could put behind her. It'd serve her right for being social for once.

But no, that would have made sense.

Instead, she stepped through the front door into the house. It was empty.

She turned immediately around and left through the front door out of the house.

It made no difference. Kayla found that she always entered through the front door, just like she had earlier that day. She repeated this over and over and until she forgot whether she was coming or going.

This time, however, the pre-med students finally left the bathroom, still entwined in each other, eyes only for each other. What luck. Of all the people at the party, they might recognize something was wrong with her. She exhaled. Her mouth was so dry she didn't have enough spit to even say hello.

The two didn't look at her. They were too busy inspecting each other. One set of hands pulled at their clothes, while a second set held their faces together. A third set roamed the exposed skin and stripped that away as well.

Kayla covered her mouth to stifle a scream. They turned, looked at her, and smiled.

She was out the front door again.

"Not that way," protested Jade.

She came back through in the blink of an eye, but this time, the pre-meds were an arm's reach from her. Kayla ducked and sprinted for the nearest open door. In this case, the bathroom.

The main guest bathroom, of course, lead to the double sliding glass door in the basement. Because of course it did. She slid the door shut. By the pool, where co-eds should have been laughing, were the pre-med students half-stripped and half-mad as they ran for her.

"Do something," whispered Jade. "You're the one who wanted out."

Kayla wiped her head and drew the Barrier sigil. A shimmer like ice crackled over the glass. Pre-med one threw themselves into it. The red smear of his remains as he slid to the ground did little to deter pre-med two, who did the same.

"We did it," said Kayla.

"Did what," said a voice behind her. Curious. Simple. Just a question with a complicated answer. "What can you do? Tell me. Show me."

Kayla turned around. The shadowed outline of the philosophy major sat on pool table and sharpened the end of a pool stick. She couldn't see his face, but she knew it was him by the tweed jacket and trilby hat. He set the blue chalk down and pushed off the mahogany of the pool table with a small hop. He walked into the diffused light under a stain-glass lamp and opened his arms out for her.

"Well?"

She couldn't have seen his face, even if it wasn't under a brimmed hat. He didn't have one. There was no identity to him beyond a shadow dressed like an asshole. How something without a mouth had so much to say was beyond her.

Kayla didn't answer him. She spotted a door at the other end of the basement, past a bar, a kitchen, and a second pool table. The only door was at least 20 yards away. She sprinted for it.

His head snapped 180 degrees, unlike the rest of his body. His knees faced the wrong way as he ran after her.

Now in theory, 20 yards would be about 60 feet, and could be covered in ten seconds for a weak runner.

In theory, that is.

The rules of reality that gave him an advantage by virtue of applying at all didn't seem to affect her. She ran twice as far than it should have taken, in what must have been half the time it should have taken to do that, and even still he was on her heels. His hand reached for her as she barreled into the door. She slammed it onto his fingers behind her. He shrieked, a piercing sound that made her flinch. His fingers, longer than his hand, clawed and scratched at the wood.

Kayla recovered with a gasp and smeared the barrier sigil on the door. He continued to tear the wood down piece by splintering piece, howling the entire time in his attempt to get to her, but the barrier held fast.

Again, if the house were the reasonable sort, she'd have been on the first floor and not the second after leaving the basement. The hallway stretched out behind her with more doors than would have fit in the length of the house. She tried to catch her shuddering breaths and leaned against the wall. No escape.

"Are you okay?" whispered Jade from deep inside her chest.

"No," spat Kayla. "You kidding?"

"Not good with parties, huh?"

"You could say that." Kayla slid down the wall and buried her head between her knees. She hadn't lost enough blood to justify it, but she felt dizzy and her legs ached.

"I never got your name," said Jade quietly.

Kayla sighed and told her. "Do you know what's going on?" she added.

"All good things require sacrifices. I'm the part of me that didn't want to go through with it, and she locked me away."

Kayla lifted her head and winced as the pain shot into her skull like a hot knife. "Go through with what?"

"We're contained to the house for now. I didn't want anyone to leave. But once I get enough energy from your friends, the First Elder will be born and released."

Kayla remembered the starless sky. So far in the mountains, they shouldn't have had light pollution. The night should have been glittering, even behind a few clouds. She trembled and held her knees tighter.

"How the hell could you do such a thing?" she screamed into her arms.

"If you found a god who answered your prayers when all others were silent, would you not welcome him with a party?"

"I can't believe you," whispered Kayla. "I had the biggest crush on you, you know? I thought you were a good person."

Jade remained silent, a warm bubble stuck in Kayla's chest. "Well. I'm here, and she's there, right?" she finally answered.

"Yeah." Kayla sighed and helped herself to her feet by leaning against the wall. "What now?"

"We find me and take me out."

Kayla took a deep breath to steel herself and glanced down the hallway. As if they'd been heard, every door in the excessively long, narrow hall opened. The English majors stepped into the frames and on cue, turned and looked at her.

"Can I sustain the barrier?" Kayla whispered seemingly to herself.

"Yes," said Jade, "but it'll cost you."

Kayla nodded, wiped the blood from her face, and drew the sigil with both hands. A small shimmer appeared around her fists like two shields. She closed her eyes and willed them bigger but felt light-headed. She found her limit and marched down the hall, shields high and middle fingers raised to the silent witnesses watching her from dark doorways. They silently filed out behind her as she passed.

Left, up the stairs to the balcony off the master bedroom, or right, down the stairs to the first floor. She had to make a choice. On the one hand, she remembered Jaiden watching out from the eye of the triangular house. On the other, the engineering majors were crawling up the stairs on all fours, as was the most efficient way.

It was an easy choice. Up to the left she went.

She shut the door behind her and breathlessly scrawled the sigil onto the door. Her knees threatened to give out and her vision tunneled. Her face felt hot and wet from the head wound.

She heard Jade's voice behind her. No, Jaiden's.

"You weren't supposed to be here. I tried to send them to stop you. Even though we've both done things you're going to regret, I'm not angry." Jaiden laughed lightly. "Don't be afraid, K. This isn't where your life ends. It's where it begins. You can be the last witness."

Kayla forced herself to stand and pressed her back against the shimmering barrier. Jaiden had changed out of her swimsuit, having found her silk blouses and pressed pants and, presumably, the hidden closet with the missing ghost of herself. The sun rose behind her through the open window to the balcony. And in the sky, a massive being descended upon the mountain and searched the ground with sweeping black tentacles.

Jaiden faced her, a frigid grin plastered on her face, her eyes sunken and wild. She marched to the nightstand next to the master bed.

"Move!" screamed Jade from inside her.

Kayla remained frozen, her breath and heart paused like time itself as she watched Jaiden pulled a pistol from the drawer. Her arm moved for her as Jade assumed direct control and signed the sigil in front of her. The bullet deflected off the shield and cracked the mirror of the vanity.

Jaiden shook her head with a chuckle and shot at Kayla's leg this time.

She thought she would scream, that she would feel pain, but she felt nothing, said nothing, as she dropped to one knee, then collapsed. The barrier disappeared. She felt...warm. It'd be so easy to sleep and wake up from what she hoped was a terrible dream. But Jade's voice hissed at her to stay awake.

"Don't leave me alone with myself," she screamed.

Kayla lifted her head and tried to push herself up on her palms. Jaiden turned her back and raised her arms to the birth of her god, silhouetted against the rising sun. Her god answered and settled before her.

Her body didn't want to move, but while Kayla breathed, she found strength. She dragged herself, arm after arm, across the wooden floor. Left, right, left, right, left, up, down, in the shape of the sigil. She wanted to punch God, such as he was, in his monstrously blank face, but this worked, too. Her task done, she sighed slowly. A small bubble of a ghost left her bleeding lips and flitted across the room. She couldn't hear Jade's voice anymore.

The world was silent as darkness enveloped the room and God watched. Jade's ghost was a pinpoint star that sunk into her other half's body, and Jaiden screamed. Kayla heard her struggle with herself as cabinets were hit and scuffles of her polished shoes scraped the floor. Warmth left Kayla, starting at her toes like she was dipped in ice water. The sigil activated with a brilliant, shimmering light that illuminated the dark bedroom.

Jaiden had thrown herself into the mirror, and struggled against her own hand, which held a shattered piece of glass over the tattoo on her chest. Her other hand pushed herself away by the wrist, but she was stronger than herself. She carved the sigil into her chest. Both her hands fell away, limp, and red seeped; stained her fine, silk blouse.

A black tendril slipped through the window and wrapped itself around Jaiden's languished body. The sigil shown over her heart and the tendril faded like smoke.

The last thing Kayla saw was the inside of her eyelids.

Time held no meaning, neither did space. A limitlessness universe existed for the human mind to explore but she knew none of it, confined by the boundaries she set for herself. What could she know that she didn't know?

So, Kayla didn't know how she woke up on the bedroom floor with her hair plastered to a sticky red mess of her own making. Coagulated blood shut her right eye as she forced herself to wake. Jaiden was kneeled beside her, a phone to one ear and holding her towel to Kayla's head. Concern painted her beautiful face and her lips spoke words to someone Kayla didn't hear.

"Did it work?" whispered Kayla, her voice hoarse in her throat.

"Yeah, she seems confused, but she's awake now, thank God," said Jaiden.

Massive head trauma or not, Kayla saw her wink.

BRILLIANT MONSTROSITY

MELISSA KOONS

She was brilliant. She was horrible. She was grotesque. But she was brilliant. No one could deny her brilliance. I admired her for it. I coveted her mind, yet I know I was blessed in my denial. That kind of mind was not a gift. It was a glorious monstrosity.

She was my friend. My only friend. I was 20 when I escaped my rural hometown in the Midwest and fled to a college town on the East coast. I wasn't enrolled, I didn't have the brains or the commitment for it—but she did. All I had was a suitcase and a backpack with all my worldly possessions in them. She called me a "survivor." She made it sound so prestigious. I never saw it that way. I was just living my life. I didn't realize that the conditions of it—up to that point—were something to be survived. I endured; that's what I thought living was. I found a run-down, studio apartment and I got a job working at the all-night diner just off campus. I didn't know much about city life—even small, college town, city life—but I could take care of myself. I always took

71

care of myself. Until I met her. Now, I consider myself a survivor.

I worked behind the bar during the graveyard and served the regulars who sat at the counter. My boss didn't want me to carry food very far, I didn't have the coordination for it. Nor the personality to charm the college kids and truckers who sat at the booths. I didn't have the adorable smile that the other 20-year-old waitress had, nor the charm of the 40-year-old waitress who'd been working there for half her life. I had the personality of a rock, and the looks to match—at least, that's what my boss said. The regulars at the counter wouldn't mind, and the chef preferred a rock to someone who would chat with him through the window. He liked silence while he worked, just like me.

But she didn't see me that way. She blustered in with a group of friends late one Friday night. Her hair was red like the blazing sunset and her smile was just as blinding. Her friends were drunk and so was she, but she maintained her dignity whereas her friends did not. They fell all over each other in the booth, their too-short skirts riding up their thighs, their laughs too loud, and their hair and make-up mussed with sweat. She was radiant. Her laugh was charming, but not gregarious; her beauty was natural and her style was modest. Her brilliance extended beyond her mind.

"Forgive my friends," she had come up to me, cash in hand. "I'm going to cover the check and get them out of here, will you make sure Sandi gets her tip?" Her eyes were bright and clear, the coffee working wonders to sober her up. She nodded her head toward the experienced waitress who practically ran the night shift.

I nodded at her mutely and took her cash, averting my gaze from hers. What good was it for the sun to shine so brightly upon a rock?

"Thank you... Ingrid." Her eyes flicked down to my nametag and she gave me a sweet smile before she left with her belligerent friends.

I was shocked she had even bothered to notice me. Not just thrown her check at me like so many others did but truly notice *me*. I was even more shocked when she came back. Every Friday night. At first it was with her friends then, as the weeks and the semester went on, she came on her own. She became another regular who sat at the bar. Veronica was her name. She brought books and papers with her. She studied voraciously, sipping coffee and eating crispy bacon while she read through chemistry text books I couldn't begin to comprehend.

"What are you working on?" I mumbled one night. I'd spent the last few weeks trying to work up the courage to ask, but I didn't want to disturb her any more than a rock would want to interrupt the sun.

Veronica looked up at me, startled and yet pleasantly surprised. "Ahh, you do speak. Well, Ingrid, I am studying the chemistry of the brain. I've just started my Master's degree and I'm trying to figure out my thesis so I can review it with my advisor at the end of the semester."

I tilted my head to the side, my brows etched into a frown. "Thesis?"

Veronica let out a soft laugh. "Sorry, the theory I am trying to prove."

I nodded dumbly. She was brilliant. But I already told you that. She went on to explain to me—with wild hand gestures and impassioned speech—how she believed she could find a cure for anxiety.

"Not a symptom treatment like all the other prescription drugs, actually *cure* anxiety."

The way she said it, I believed her. I had no reason not to. It all seemed so grand to me and I had no doubt that her brilliant mind would be able to cure anything she wanted to. "How?"

She grinned. It was a wide, beaming grin that put the dawn to shame. "Chemistry. The brain releases a chemical response from the amygdala through the limbic system that triggers a fight or flight response to a perceived danger."

I gave her a confused look, hardly comprehending what she was saying.

"Sorry," she cleared her throat. "I get so excited I forget that normal people have no idea what I'm talking about." She chuckled. I warmth spread through me at the realization she thought me normal. Not boring, not dull, not a rock—normal.

"The amygdala is a part of the brain that's in charge of processing fear. Its job it to help us survive by alerting us to a dangerous situation so we can fight it or run away from it. Anxiety disorders, though, mean the individual is hypersensitive to filtering situations through their fear processing system and their brain releases the chemical for a fear response even when there's nothing scary happening."

I nodded along, barely following her but not wanting her to stop talking. She was the first person to actually believe I could understand something as complex as what she was explaining. She wasn't talking down to me, yelling at me, abusing me. She was communicating with me as an equal. She was the only person to ever do that in my life—which is why I went along with her grotesque and horrific destruction. How could I walk away? How could I return to a life of being a comely rock in an all-night diner, leaving my brilliant friend who treated me as her equal behind? Back to a life of squalor and pain on a farm in the Midwest. Back to being alone, forgotten, and ignored.

"I propose that we can alter the chemistry in the brain—not just to block the chemistry that triggers anxiety, but to actually correct it. I think I can re-balance the brain." She said with glee.

I should have known it couldn't be done. "That sounds complicated," I muttered.

"Well sure, but I've got a good hypothesis. I just need to test it out," she looked over her notes and bit her lip in concentration. She glanced up from the page in her hand and narrowed her eyes at me critically, pursing her lips as she pondered. "Would you like to help me?"

My shock stopped my breath in my throat and I choked on it. I shook my head and my eyes went wide. Me? Help? Why would she think I would be capable of such a thing? "I-I don't know anything about that. I don't have, I mean, I haven't studied science or anything—"

"Oh, don't worry about that. I'll take care of all the chemistry stuff," she assured me.

"But I don't have anxiety, I don't think…" I mumbled, looking down at my fingers which I twisted awkwardly around each other.

"That's okay, because I do."

My head snapped up and I sputtered a little in my surprise. Her? Anxiety? But she seemed so perfect. So composed. So… unblemished. "You?" I whispered, trying to wrap my mind around it.

She laughed. A sweet, delicate laugh. "Yes, me. You don't have to look so astonished, it's a very common condition that affects nearly 18 percent of the nation's population."

"Oh," I answered dumbly. 18 didn't seem like a very big number to me, but the way she said made it sound like it was. I believed her. I should have believed her more. I learned just how large a number 18 could be when referring to groups of millions.

"Are you interested?" She asked, her smiling pulling me in with its innocent excitement. I should have said "no."

I looked around her lab and twisted my fingers anxiously in front of my chest. It was pristine. It was clean, organized, and I was terrified to touch anything. My head twitched in jerky motions as I took it all in. The smooth counters, the sparkling beakers, the leather chair positioned beside an IV and several needles connected to vials with bright, neon fluid. I gulped and looked away from it; the computer with line charts and graphs, a heart rate monitor beeping, needles, needles, needles.

"Don't worry, I'll be the only one getting injected," Veronica chuckled, walking toward the needles and fiddling with them. Her white, lab coat made her blend in with the counters and walls; her motions seemed almost invisible as she prepared the dosages.

"Alright," I whispered, taking a cautionary step closer toward her.

"What I need from you, Ingrid, is to monitor my vitals—that's the heart rate machine over here. If my heart gets too high—above 100—or too low—below 40—I need you to stop the injections." She pointed to the screen and the numbers on it that I was supposed to monitor.

"Okay, what do I do if something bad happens?" I asked nervously.

Veronica whipped around and grinned at me. "Pray that nothing does."

She walked over to the injectors and pointed to the neon tubes. "Once I'm all hooked up, we will count down from three. At one, I want you to push down the plunger on each syringe. It will inject the solution into the tube that I'll insert into my vein," she turned to me then, her hand hovering over the first plunger. "Ingrid, it's very important that you push these down in order. Left to right."

Her smile faded and the seriousness in her eyes was unlike anything I'd seen before. I nodded emphatically. "Yes, I understand. Left to right."

"Good. Once you start a dosage, you must inject all of it into my veins."

I nodded even though my brow furrowed in confusion. "But you said to stop it if your heart rate gets too high or low."

"Yes, but only stop after you've finished the dosage. We can halt the process in between the chemicals, but the dosages are very precise and if the full amount isn't given there could be side effects." She leveled me with a very serious stare.

"Okay. Left to right, push it all the way down." I recited.

"Perfect." Her smile returned and she walked away, toward the lab room door. She stripped off her lap coat and hung it on a peg.

"Let's get started then."

I nodded, twisting my fingers some more.

She took a seat in the chair, her feet propped up and the seatback reclined. She took the IV tube and butterfly needle attached to it. Using her left hand, she tapped the skin on the inside of her elbow, her arm outstretched. When she found her vein, she slid the butterfly needle into her arm and pressed it there. A little bit of blood went up into the tube before it went back down. "Got it. Can you put some medical tape over it to hold it there?"

I scrambled to do ask she asked, my hand shaking as I did.

"Hey, Ingrid," she stopped me, resting her left hand over mine as I pressed the tape down over the IV line. "It's okay," she said, reassuring me.

I released a shaky breath and nodded. I took a step back, checking the heart rate monitor as she instructed. "Okay, ready."

"Three..." Veronica started, staring at me.

I moved toward the first plunger of six.

"Two..."

I hovered my hand over it, willing it to be steady.

"One."

I pressed down on the plunger, moving quickly to the next one and the next. Left to right, all the way down. The heart monitor began to beep rapidly, her heart rate increased with each vial that was injected into her bloodstream. 60. 67. 78. I kept pushing them down: left to right, all the way down. 93. 101. As I reached the final plunger, Veronica started convulsing. I gasped and looked at the heart monitor. 120. Way too high.

I panicked, looking around and unsure what to do. I thrust the final plunger down, using only half the force as I ran to her side to restrain her so that she didn't fall off the chair. My arm got wrapped in the IV line and as I bent over her I pulled the IV from her arm. Green fluid splashed on the floor, the tube not yet emptied into her bloodstream. Blood dripped down her arm but I ignored it, working instead to hold her shoulders down until her body stopped convulsing. I prayed over and over in my mind. My lips moved silently around the words, wishing them all to come true. Please let her be okay. Please let her come through this. Please don't let me have killed my only friend.

I should have let death claim her. It would have been more merciful—for everyone.

After an eternity of seconds, her body stopped its spasms and she lay still. Her eyes were closed and her breathing normalized. I watched the heart rate monitor closely as the number started to come down to a safer level. When it hit 80, her eyes fluttered open.

Veronica stared up at the ceiling. She blinked rapidly, adjusting her eyes to the blindingly white room. She swallowed with some difficulty.

I scooted off her, grabbed her bottled water and held it out to her. She took it with her left hand, popping the top with her thumb and took a long drink. Once she gulped down nearly half the bottle she handed it back to me. Her eyes noticed the bright colors swirling on the floor: a vibrant, green serum and deep, red blood intermingling like a holiday card on the floor. Her eyes trailed up from the floor to her arm where the wound at her elbow was clotting and the congealed blood around the puncture mark stopped dripping. Her blue eyes continued their trail up her arm and over to the syringes where all six plungers were pushed down.

"Did you finish it?" She asked, her voice hoarse.

I nodded.

She looked back down at the milliliters of serum on the floor—a seemingly inconsequential amount. "Good."

I hadn't seen or heard from Veronica for a week after the experiment. I looked for her at the counter when I got to the diner each night, but she wasn't there. Each time the door opened and the bell *dinged* during my shift, my heart stopped. I would look up from whatever I was doing, holding my breath in hopes that it was her. It wasn't. I worried about her, the green serum tie-dyed with blood on the floor was all I could see when I closed my eyes. I prayed she was okay. She was, and yet, never would be again.

When she did finally return, I didn't notice her come in.

"Come on, baby. I'll tip ya real nice," a trucker leered at Kim, the typically cheerful waitress. He grabbed at her apron, trying to pull her closer to the table.

Her face was twisted in fear and disgust as she tried to wriggle out of his grasp. She held the coffee pot out like a weapon, but her frown told me she was conflicted between defending herself and keeping her job. If she bashed his head in, that wouldn't be considered good customer service.

I was terrified to confront the trucker on my own. He was a large man; both tall and wide. His fingers were thick and callused, snagging the canvas material of her apron on his rough skin. But his eyes were the most terrifying. The almond shape of them made them appear small in his round face, and his pupils were constricted in the harsh florescent bulbs—like pin pricks on a brown canvas. They brought back memories of another man—much larger than myself—with almond shaped eyes that looked too small for his face. His booming voice and violent hands crashed down upon me when I couldn't meet his expectations. His unattainable expectations that he held for maintaining a home in the Midwest.

The trucker terrified me; the memories of my home haunted me. I couldn't confront him, but I couldn't allow him to continue his assault on Kim. I moved around the counter and darted to the back room for the manager. "Kim needs help." I told him bluntly, not waiting to see if he was following me before I dashed back to the front.

That was the night Veronica returned. I came around the corner and she was standing there, between Kim and the handsy trucker. I froze behind her. She looked fearless. Her blue eyes were chilling and her red hair tumbled over her shoulders like fiery waves. Her shoulders were squared and her fists balled at her sides.

The trucker sneered at her, but she didn't falter. He had no effect on her.

"I said, back the fuck off." Veronica spat.

"What ya gonna do about it? Yer just a pretty young thing. I could show ya a thing or two," the trucker chuckled, reaching out to touch her hair.

Without hesitation, Veronica grabbed his wrist and twisted it, wrenching his arm back and making him squeal in pain.

"That's enough!" My manager shouted, darting between the two and making Veronica release the trucker. "I want you both gone before I call the police!"

Veronica snorted but turned around anyway, not bothering to argue with the manager. Her eyes met mine as she strode toward the door. A smile curved the corners of her lips. She brushed past me, silent as sin.

If the trucker's eyes had frightened me, the look in hers shook me to my core. His were lecherous and overpowering. Hers held nothing. There was no fear. No concern. No recognition of what she had done. Only a smile and a hardened determination I didn't know how to interpret.

"The man known as Adam Wesley has gone missing. He works as a truck driver for Atlantic Shipping Co. and failed to meet his check point in Virginia two days ago. If you have seen this man, please call your local authorities."

The news flashed a picture of a familiar round face and almond shaped eyes. I inhaled sharply and averted my gaze, blocking it out.

"Let's change the channel, shall we?" Kim said, coming up to the counter and searching for the remote to the TV. She found it under the counter and flipped the channel to an old sitcom, her shoulders visibly relaxing now that the trucker's face was no longer plastered above her section. "I had rather hoped when he left here a week ago that would be the last I saw of his face."

I nodded and remained silent.

Kim glanced over at me, looking at me—really looking at me—for the first time. "Thank your friend for me the next time you see her."

I nodded again, not sure when that would be. I hadn't heard from her since her attack on the trucker, and she hadn't tried to come back.

"And I should thank you for getting Paul. It's nice to know you've got my back," she grinned at me and patted me on the shoulder before returning to her section and the customers she had sitting there.

A small smile graced my face. I scanned the diner, taking an inventory of our customers and any refills. Through the windows, my eyes caught sight of a flash of familiar red hair. I looked closer and just beyond my plain reflection in the window was the vision of Veronica. I blinked once and she vanished. I stared quizzically at the door, uncertain if I had really seen her or not.

The door opened, the little bell hanging above it chimed and broke me from my concentration. A familiar face walked through the door, smiling at me. Panic rose in my breast and clenched around my heart, squeezing it and making it pump faster. I recalled what Veronica had told me about the amygdala and in that moment oh how I wished I could make it stop pumping chemicals into my limbic system. How I wished I could temper my fear response. How I wished I could stand tall and fearless, like she did the night she confronted the trucker. Sometimes it can be a blessing not to have wishes granted. It was a curse that my prayers in the lab had been.

"Found you," he whispered, sitting down at the bar in front of me. He was tall, and wide. His almond shaped eyes were fixed on mine, his pupils constricted—pin pricks on a hazel canvas. His broad shoulders hunched as he leaned in toward me, the grin still stretched across his face. "So this is where you've been, Ingrid."

My hands shook and I took a step back, wiping my sweaty palms on my apron. He couldn't be here. He shouldn't be here. It was a vision. The trucker returned. It couldn't be him. How did he find me? I had been so careful. I took everything I had with me, and left everything and everyone else behind. My eyes flicked down to his large fists resting on the counter. I knew those fists, and I knew how they could hurt.

"You've had your fun in the city. It's time to come home," he said, standing up and stretching his arm out to me.

I shook my head.

"This is no way for a wife to behave toward her husband. Come with me, Ingrid."

I shook my head again.

He narrowed his eyes at me. "I won't say it again."

I glanced over at Kim. She was busy laughing with one of the customers, trying to charm him into giving her a bigger tip. It was no use. My eyes scanned all the patrons and none seemed to notice the dangerous man at the counter. Perhaps he was only dangerous to me. My eyes swept over the windows and latched on to a smile gleaming on the other side of the glass.

"Going on break," I told the chef behind the window. I didn't bother to take my apron off. I wouldn't be gone long. Or so I had thought.

"That'a girl."

I followed my estranged husband out of the diner knowing that a brilliant scientist was waiting for us. She would have my back, just like she had Kim's. Believing that gave me hope as I followed him into the dark.

He led me toward his old Volvo in the parking lot, not pausing to see if I was behind him because there was no doubt in his mind that I would be. I only followed him because I knew that she followed us as the sun follows night. Her fearless smile gave me strength.

"Get in," he commanded, unlocking the passenger side door first.

I didn't even get a chance to open my mouth. She was there. Veronica leapt on him, swinging a tire iron down upon his head. He let out a single yelp and then was silent as she brought the iron down again and again. Blood splattered upward and out, spraying over the car, the gravel, my apron, her face. It blended into her hair and there was so much I wasn't sure where her natural color ended and the blood began.

She stopped her assault after three blows and took a step back, kicking his leg with her toe to see if he was still conscious. Or alive.

He remained still, the back of his head concave and gray matter visible beneath his fractured skull.

"What have you done?" I asked, looking up at her blood-splattered face.

She smiled at me; her grotesque, horrible, fearless smile. "You don't have to deal with him anymore."

"What did you do!" I cried, looking down at his slaughtered body. "How?" I gasped, shaking my head as dread set in.

She was unfazed. There was no dread, no worry, no remorse. "What? Didn't you want to be free of him?" She took a step toward me, her hand gripping the tire iron tighter. "Just like Kim wanted to be free from the truck driver."

My face contorted into a disgusted frown. "Kim's trucker?" I took a step back.

"Yes, the man who had you so frightened. I understand now, the resemblance in their eyes and expressions was uncanny." Veronica said, looking down at my husband's bashed in face. "Well, they were before, anyway." She pushed his cheek in with her toe, tilting his head to look at his glassy and wide eyes.

"I can fix that, you know?" She said suddenly, looking up from his corpse to my horrified face.

"Fix what? How can you fix this! He's dead. They're both dead!" I was getting hysterical and her unflappable demeanor was more fearsome than my husband ever was.

She let out a laugh, that beautiful laugh. "Oh no, I meant I can fix your fear." She closed the distance between us so quickly I didn't have a chance to turn and run. She grabbed my wrist and pulled me close to her; her face was so close our noses nearly touched and her breath was hot, moist upon my cheek.

"It worked, Ingrid." Her eyes blazed with a triumphant brilliance. "It worked!"

"What did?" I whispered, my body shivering though it wasn't cold. Her grasp around me was an unbreakable vice and my skin turned white from the pressure of her fingers.

"The experiment. My serum worked! It cured my anxiety—more than that, it cured my fear." Her grin widened, she ignored the sirens moving toward us down the interstate.

I glanced over my shoulder back at the diner. Horrified faces were pressed against the window, watching us. Kim had her hand over her mouth and tears streamed down her cheeks. My manager, held a phone in his hand as he locked the door. Locking them in. Keeping us out. They stared at her and I the same, with equal horror and equal blame. They didn't have my back. But she did.

"Come with me, Ingrid."

I stared into her brilliant face. Her horrible eyes. Her grotesque smile. What had I helped create? This brilliant scientist, now without fear who saved others without hope. Who massacred the powerful and brought them to their knees with a twinkle in her eye and a laugh on her breath. She was brilliant. She was horrible. She was grotesque. She was a monster. A brilliant monster.

"Come with me and we'll cure the world of fear."

"Yes," I whispered, gripping her wrist in a bond I could never escape. She was my master, my keeper, my friend.

Veronica's grin brightened with excitement and she pulled me away, into the darkness. Her hair illuminated the path like a sunbeam, and I was too captivated not to follow. 18 percent of the nation's population. 18 percent of millions. She was going to make them all like her. She was horrible. She was grotesque. She was a brilliant monstrosity.

ESOPHAGEAL FOREIGN BODY
THOMAS A. FOWLER

I sat in the emergency room waiting area, feeling more spit gathering in my mouth. Trying to swallow, the spit went nowhere, holding its position firmly in my throat. I hocked into my silver, to-go coffee mug, slowly filling it with more mucus.

"Sorry about this," the technician said. "The printer almost never acts up."

I watched as the technician, trying to onboard me, unplugged the phone cable then put it back in place to see if that reestablished the connection to the computer. My thumb tapped the cup, waiting for them to get me in.

"You said your airway isn't blocked," the technician said with a questioning inflection.

"Yeah, I can breathe. I just can't..." I coughed. "I just can't swallow."

"Okay, still this can't be comfortable. Moving as fast as I can to get you in to get your digestive track free and clear," the technician said.

"I understand," I said. "You're doing what you can." I looked at the technician's name tag. "Benjamin. Do you go by Benjamin? Or Ben?"

"Benjamin," he replied.

I coughed again. As the spit collected my throat rejected the buildup. I brought my coffee mug below my mouth, hocking like a cat with a hairball to eject. I coughed more, feeling the piece of steak tightly lodged in my throat. I never thought I'd be able to feel how each muscle within my throat moved when I coughed, but the stuck food made the path so tight; every movement from my cough was adamantly apparent. Heat rushed through my body, blood surged in my head as the air tightened. Spit collected in the mug.

"Are you okay?" Benjamin asked.

The scratch in my throat; I didn't want to talk. I just nodded instead, giving an "okay" hand gesture. Bringing my head back, I felt something warm and wet on my shirt.

"Oh, jeez," Benjamin said. He looked around for a tissue or napkin. He grabbed his late-night dinner, in a Styrofoam container, and pulled a napkin he hadn't used yet. "Here you go."

I wiped the drool off my shirt and shoulder. Embarrassed, I shook my head, hating that I'd been so stupid to get a piece of steak stuck in my throat. Was I a child who couldn't chew his food? Was I that big of a moron that now I'd be paying $1,000 just to finish getting a piece of beef into my stomach?

"Tell you what, let me get the nurse, see if she can get you back there while I figure out this printer issue," Benjamin said. He grabbed a phone, dialing the back area. The phone on the other side of the entrance doors rang. "Hi, this printer won't work. Can you come help Mr. Crowler out, even though I haven't finished onboarding?"

"Crowley," I clarified.

"Mr. Crowley, my apologies," Benjamin said. "Okay, thank you."

Benjamin hung up. I felt the piece of steak move. It was subtle, but since things were never meant to remain in your throat it didn't take much sensation to notice any changes.

"She's coming. Can you leave your ID and insurance card?" Benjamin put the paper I filled out by hand on a clip board. He centered the papers. "I'll bring them back to you as soon as I can get this done."

I nodded, worried talking would cause me to cough and spit-up more, so I decided to keep quiet whenever I could. I handed my cards over, Benjamin placed them under the metal clip of the board then went straight back to the printer.

"Hi there," a woman said.

"Hi," Benjamin said. "This is Aaron Crowley."

"Not Crowler," the woman said.

Benjamin worked on the printer, resetting the power without stopping a beat. "Yes, he was eating some steak and it's been stuck in his throat…"

"Almost two and a half hours now," I said. A quick cough, trying to avoid another major spell.

The nurse ushered me out of the chair and toward the entrance. We spoke as we made our way into the emergency room. She was petite, just a few inches over five feet, her hair had some gray, her eyes a deep brown.

"What's your insurance?" the nurse asked.

"Kreshner," I said.

"They didn't send you to afterhours urgent care?" she asked.

"They close at 8," I replied.

"Not really an afterhours clinic, then, is it?" she said. "We're turning right, then headed into room eleven."

I followed her instructions. "No, should be called, For-Issues–Shortly-After-Work Care," I said.

"I'll have to remember that one," she said.

Too much talking. I felt the mucus try to work past the steak to no avail. I coughed. My face turned red, the pain in my throat seared with each constriction struggling against the unnatural pressure.

"Whoa, alright, let's get you on the bed," the nurse said.

I sat, not falling back until I had hocked up everything that had built up.

"Before you sit back, let's ditch the coat," the nurse said. "That way we can check your blood pressure and probably set up a drip pretty soon, here."

I spit one more time. It was thick, making me wipe some residue clinging to my lip, I slid it on the edge of the mug, trying to usher it to the bottom of the cup.

"Still breathing okay?" she asked.

I nodded.

"Not great though, right?" she added.

I nodded.

"Okay, let me see if the doctor is free," the nurse said. She filled a cup of water and put it on the tray next to the hospital bed. Stepping out, she paused at the entrance. "I'm Emilia, by the way. I'm here for the next hour and fifteen minutes, then we're getting a rotation, but I'll help you out until then. Hopefully we can both leave about the same time, or you beat me out of here, okay?"

I nodded.

"We'll get you taken care of." She smiled and left.

I placed my coat on the chair. I removed my wallet from my back pocket and placed it in my coat, so I wasn't resting on it the whole time in the hospital bed. I took the cup of water, trying the smallest sip.

Please work, I thought. *I'd love to just have this water do the trick, for some reason, and get the hell out of here!*

The sip started fine. It moved down my tongue and into my throat no problem. Then "the fun" began. I felt the water stop, resting where the steak clung inside my throat. I let it sit, breathing through my nose, seeing if the water would somehow get through and help the steak slide. There was a slight trickle. The subtle movement of a few drops of water through my digestive track. After that, I felt my spit accumulate again, building. I spewed it all into my mug.

Angered, I decided to try making myself throw up again. I put my finger down my throat. I gagged. More spit. Nothing else. I deliberately coughed, trying to get the steak to move. Nothing.

I sat back, accepting I'd done what I could. Now it was time to relax and let them do what they could; accepting I was about to pay hundreds, if not thousands, because I was an idiot. Several minutes passed. It didn't surprise me. Of all the people in an emergency room, I was likely the last of their worries.

The steak moved. Only a little. I groaned, putting my hand against my neck, hoping it would reduce the pain somehow. It didn't. The solid pressure of something foreign in my throat pushed against my esophagus. I tried swallowing. Nothing moved. I spit a little into my mug. Once the pressure of the steak moving stopped, I tried softly massaging my throat, anything to get it moving or to relieve the tight, anguish making camp in my body. I groaned again, this time not out of pain, but out of anger. I felt exactly where the steak was stuck by the vibrations caused from my groan.

Emilia knocked, and stepped back in. The doctor accompanied her. "Hello, Aaron. This is Doctor Pineda."

"Hi," I said.

"All right," Pineda said. "Sorry you're spending your evening here, but it's nice to meet you, regardless. So, we're classifying this as an Esophageal Foreign Body. Which is fancy doctor-speak for 'some crap's stuck in your throat.'"

I smiled for the first time in hours. The doctor, in her late thirties, Hispanic, had her dark hair in a pony-tail. She had a vibrant, key-lime shirt on under the doctor's coat.

"Piece of steak, if I'm not mistaken?" Pineda said.

I nodded.

"That's a common one, just glad it's only in your G.I. track, otherwise you'd be visiting us in very different circumstances," Pineda said.

"G.I.?" I asked.

"Joe. Real American Hero." Pineda laughed, putting gloves on. "Sorry, it's the gastro-intestinal track. Because it's stuck there, instead of your air duct, that's the reason you can breathe. Had it gone down 'the wrong tube,' as so many say it, you would've had to have gotten here a lot quicker."

She brought her hands around my neck, she gently pushed against the skin, feeling around. "Bit more pressure now." Her fingers pushed in further. "Can you tell me where it is? Above the esophagus? Below?"

"Just below, right around the bottom area of my Adam's apple, I think," I said.

"Not really feeling it," Pineda said. "But that's beside the point for the time being. Can we get a drip going?"

Emilia went right for the silver cabinet.

"We're going to start with a drug that acts as an intense muscle relaxer, your throat and muscles are likely quite tense and strained from all the struggle. I like the first step to be the easiest one. If it relaxes enough, we'll have you drink some pop, which often helps urge it down. If it doesn't, we'll have to call over the GI specialist to try some of their sorcerer's ways."

I cleared my throat, or at least tried. "What might that be?"

"Well, we'll start with a scan, determine size, location. With foreign bodies and the digestive system, there's really only two ways to go. They'll either use a tube to vacuum it out, essentially, or help usher it in your stomach—where it should've gone in the first place."

I took in a strong breath through my nostrils. My lips closed together, and I slowly exhaled to relax.

Pineda, seeing my tension, shrugged. "But, hey! Let's solve this with the muscle relaxer and some soda pop, then we won't have to worry about it. You'll just have to deal with our smiling faces, am I right?"

"That does sound better." I coughed.

"Absolutely it does," Pineda said. "We'll give the Metaxalone some time, then we'll try some big gulps. Probably won't feel great, but if we can get that steak into your stomach without scans and tubes, then it'll be worth it."

"Sure," I said.

Pineda left. I turned toward Emilia as she swabbed my arm with a wipe.

"Metaxalone?" I asked.

"That's the muscle relaxer," she said.

I nodded.

"Poke coming in 3, 2..."

Emilia stopped counting, the pinch of the needle going through the skin took over the countdown in my head. I thought the pain was done. But as she put the tape on, it caused the needle to shift a little. I felt it bump to the right.

"I moved it a bit, didn't I?" Emilia asked.

"You're fine," I replied.

"I appreciate it," Emilia said. "Sorry about that. Can I get you anything?"

I shook my head, smiling to show her all was well.

"I'm going to grab the Metaxalone, and be back in a few," she said.

She returned with a soda in hand and a vial of medicine, along with a small handheld plunger to administer the medicine into my drip.

"You'll feel a really cold sensation when I first put this in. It'll take only a few seconds, then it'll pass. Nothing to worry about." Emilia readied the plunger. "You won't feel an immediate relaxation, the Metaxalone will need to work its way through your system a bit."

She placed a control on the bed next to me. "This controls your TV, if anything changes or you need me, just press this button. That'll let me know to come by. Otherwise, we'll try some big sips of soda in about twenty minutes."

She put the plunger into the drip. "Cold sensation coming your way."

I shivered. It was different from being in a blizzard or cold wind. With freezing temperatures, you felt the chill on your skin, working its way into your body. This was the opposite. A frigid sensation surged through my veins, starting in my right arm and working its way through my body. My skin reacted with goosebumps, like an explosive chill urging its way out. I shivered, but tried to keep still to avoid Nurse Emilia bumping the needle or the plunger falling out before she finished pushing the fluid in.

"Weird," I said.

As the chill dissipated, pressure in my throat increased. It felt like my throat closed more, or the steak grew somehow. I brought my left hand up to my throat.

"Feeling tightness?" Emilia asked.

I nodded my head.

"The cold might have caused some muscle constriction as a response to the temperature change. Give it a few seconds," Emilia said. She pulled the plunger, tossing it into the biohazard bin. She stood by me, waiting. "Any better?"

"I think so," I replied.

"I'm going to check on other patients, I'll be back in a bit after this has done its job." Emilia left the room.

Keeping my hand on my throat, it gave me some comfort, almost like putting your arm in a sling after injuring it. Providing some pressure and relief felt better.

I felt movement. My esophagus? Was the muscle relaxer taking effect? It didn't hurt as much but, nonetheless, the piece of steak moved.

I looked over at the soda. Would attempting it now be that bad? I'd tried only sips of water before and that didn't work. Not like I'd drink the entire can. Worse thing that would happen was nothing changed.

I grabbed the can and pulled the tab. The snap of the aluminum cracked through the room, followed by the carbonation fizzing out. Just before I took a sip, I got rid of any mucous buildup. I walked over to the sink, just in case I puked or something. I dumped my coffee mug first, giving the muscle relaxer a few more moments, seeing if there was any more movement.

Washing the mug out, I grimaced as the spit— accumulated from almost three hours of gagging and hocking—went into the sink and down the drain.

A knock came from behind.

"Hi, heard the pop can open," Pineda said.

"Yeah," I replied. "Felt some movement, was thinking of at least trying."

"Hey, if you're feeling up to it, worse thing that happens is nothing," she said.

"That's what I was thinking," I said. I almost took a sip but hesitated out of fear nothing would change. "Where are you from?"

"Mid-west. Chicago originally. You?" she asked.

"Born in Massachusetts, lived here for a long time, though," I said.

"Did the 'pop' give me away?" Pineda asked.

I nodded.

"I figured you weren't originally from here, 'soda' isn't too common, either," she added.

I coughed. Felt more movement, like the steak was drifting farther. I took in a big breath from my nose, exhaled slowly through my lips.

"If you're feeling movement that's good, the 'soda' should help," Pineda said.

"Thanks, I'm just nervous. Nervous..."

"It won't work?" said Pineda.

I nodded.

"You'll be okay," Pineda said.

I put a huge gulp in my mouth. Before trying to swallow, I let the soda sit there, getting ready like swallowing a huge pill. The carbonation popped in my mouth. Swallowing took a concerted effort; my mouth rejected the idea at first.

Then I tried again. It moved to the back of my throat, flowing into my digestive track. It all stopped. I felt movement. The steak was moving down. It froze. Tiny tinges of pain hit the walls of my digestive track. Every ounce of soda flew out of my mouth into the sink.

Pineda patted my back. "You okay?"

I didn't answer, I kept coughing. More soda flew out, mixed with spit and mucous. The tinge didn't go away.

"Aaron? Do you prefer Aaron or Mr. Crowley?" she asked.

"Aaron, please." More soda. I turned on the water, not wanting Doctor Pineda to see everything now in the sink. Reaching for the sink handle, I stopped. The piece of steak.

"What?" I said.

"Huh?" Pineda asked. She looked in the sink. "Oh, great! That's amazing! Not the direction I expected things to go, figured it'd head south for the winter. But, glad for the outcome."

"Still feels like it's in there," I said.

"Well, probably the muscles reacting, they went through a lot tonight, more than usual," she said.

I grabbed the can, taking another sip. The soda stopped again. I coughed it all up, but this time no more steak, just soda and spit.

"Might be another piece, unfortunately," Pineda said.

"Everyone okay?" Emilia entered the room.

"Got some out, seems to be more than just the one piece though," Pineda said.

I shook my head in confusion.

"I was only a few bites in, how could…" I stopped. The tiny tinges of pain, like a rough patch of cactus pricks, got stronger. I began coughing harder as the pressure increased.

"Aaron? Aaron what's going on?" Pineda asked.

"Pressure's getting worse," I replied. "Much worse."

"Does it feel like your chest is getting tighter? Harder to breathe?" Pineda asked.

I nodded.

"Both?" Pineda said.

I nodded.

"Hop back on the bed. Take your mug." Pineda turned her attention from me. "Emilia, I need Doctor Maron over here immediately. Let him know about the situation, I'm not digging this. Prep a camera and get suction tubes and oxygen intubation ready in case we need it. If pressure increases or his oxygen gets cut off, we may have to move fast."

Pineda handed me the can. "Can you try one more time? For some reason pop's helped people get through this, not sure if it's the carbonation or the ingredients. Let's try a big gulp, if we can nip this quick, I want to, okay?"

I nodded. Pineda grabbed the can, helping to urge it back. It was the first time I flat out choked. I couldn't swallow, the soda collected in my mouth, nothing to be done about it. The soda spewed from my mouth, upward and outward.

"Okay, okay, bad direction on my part. Go ahead and get it all out," Pineda said.

Emilia returned, helping keep me still. I tried to keep my body from convulsing, but the involuntary coughs sent jolts through my body. Deep breath through my nose.

"Can you still breathe?" Pineda asked.

I nodded. I felt something move below the blockage.

"What's our ETA on Doctor Maron?" Pineda asked.

"On his way, about four to five minutes," answered Emilia.

It felt like a tongue. Something moved below the blockage—like a tongue cleaning teeth.

"Aaron, what's happening?" Emilia asked. "I see it in your face, something's up. Talk us through what you're feeling."

"Something is moving. Not like the piece of steak is moving through my digestive track." I brought my hand to my throat. "It's like something is moving around."

"Like it's alive?" Emilia asked.

I nodded.

"Mouth open, say ahh." Pineda tilted my head back, shining a flashlight down my throat.

I tried saying "ahh," but my throat wouldn't allow it. The cough became violent.

"Okay, don't do it if it's causing problems, but let me take a look down there," Pineda said.

I cleared my throat.

"Massive inflammation, discoloration from agitation. Can't make out any foreign bodies," Pineda said.

A surge of pain. I pressed my hand against the base of my throat, almost reaching the collar bone, it was that low. Then I felt it. A kick. Something moved so hard I felt my throat shift.

My hand trembled out of nervousness as I took Doctor Pineda's hand. Guiding it to my neck, I placed her palm to experience what I was feeling. She shook her head, feeling nothing. Then another bump. A second kick. Her eyes shot wide open.

"Okay, we have something moving in his throat. Definitely alive. Do you have any idea how this could've happened?" Pineda asked. "What it could be?"

"I was just eating a steak," I replied. "A damned steak."

"Emilia, page Doctor Maron, need him here now. See if Doctor Berthiaume is still here, too," Pineda said.

"Prep surgery?" Emilia asked.

"Check capacity, if I give the signal, it means a Rapid Response team," Pineda said.

The "tongue" grew. It expanded, pushing my digestive track against the walls of my neck. I tried screaming. The sound didn't come out, it was cut off from escaping by whatever lived in my throat. Then came sharp tacks, small incision-like piercings inside my neck. Twig-like limbs darted around. I flailed my hands, trying to reach into my throat to pull this thing out myself.

Pineda and incoming nurses stopped me. I mouthed "Get it out. Get it out," unable to speak. "It's crawling around. Get it the hell out."

"Forceps," said Pineda.

A nurse reached into the cabinet. "Obstetric?" he asked.

"Um, let's start with Hemostatic, longest we've got," Pineda replied.

The nurse nearly threw the forceps over to Pineda. The doctor stopped for a moment.

"I'm going to do this as safely as I can," Pineda said. "I can't promise I won't cause some damage or extreme pain, but seems like that's already happening with whatever's in there, yes?"

I forcibly pointed my index finger at my mouth and neck. "Go."

The limbs moved up and down, I could feel some clawing at the base of my tongue, others were pushing at the top of my chest. The tongue portion continued to grow, slithering in my digestive track as it wriggled around.

She pushed the ends of the forceps closed, keeping the body as thin as possible for entry. I gagged. Before I convulsed to puke, I pushed my body back against the hospital bed. Pineda moved the cold metal into the top of my mouth, the ends pushing against my uvula.

I gagged.

"Suction!" Pineda shouted.

A nurse moved a small suction tube into my mouth. I felt the saliva extracted out from the pressurized air. I could hear multiple people shouting. New voices entered the room. I knew I heard Emilia, but all I could focus on was not gagging and avoiding spasms as my body wanted so desperately to throw-up from the forceps and suction tube. This was Pineda's chance to get this thing out, whatever it was. I had to give Pineda the chance to pull it out.

The ends of the forceps opened, scarping against the sides of my digestive track. They closed; I felt one of the limbs struggling, its pointed ends trying to dig their way into my flesh and get free from the forceps.

"I've got it," Pineda said. "I've got..."

She stopped talking, clamping the forceps together harder. I felt the bottom limbs pull to break free. The tongue-part of its body twisted like an alligator with prey in its mouth. It spun in frantic circles.

I could taste the rubber glove with Pineda's fingers and knuckles in my mouth. She pinched her fingers tightly together, pulling.

"I've got it, extracting," Pineda said.

A nurse had a bedpan ready for everything coming up.

"No," Pineda said.

The forceps shot up quickly. They were sure, free because the limb tore off. Her hand slipped out of my mouth. Emilia grabbed Pineda to stop her from falling as her body flew back from the sudden lack of resistance. An insect-like limb flailed in the forceps. Tan blood surged from my mouth and I choked on it. I turned to my side to let it eject out. The limbs flailed in my track. The tongue moved down.

"Oh my god," I said. "It's moving toward my stomach." I took my fingers, thrusting them against the base of my throat, using the juncture where the collarbones met as a guide. I tried to stop it from moving. "There's a main body." I coughed, trying to tell them what to do. "It feels like a huge tongue." I coughed more, tan blood up as it squirted from the creature's torn limb.

"If we get that, you think we can get it out?" Pineda asked.

I nodded.

"Obstetric forceps," Pineda ordered. "Maron, head to surgery. If this doesn't work, we're meeting you down there."

"Page Rapid Response?" Maron asked.

"Absolutely," Pineda confirmed.

The forceps were huge, meant to pull a baby from a woman's body. She coated it in a lubricant, readying it to go down my throat.

"I need restraint, please," Pineda said. Nurses gathered on either side of me, putting their hands on my shoulders and arms to keep me down. "Aaron, this is going to hurt like hell but this is our last chance before it gets in your stomach. I'm going to have the nurses hold you down because your body isn't going to like this."

She hesitated. The ends of the forceps lingered at the top of my mouth.

"What are you waiting for?" a nurse asked.

"Wondering if we just go to surgery," Pineda said.

She moved the forceps closer, the ends of the metal quivering against my lips. The lubricant tasted like rubbing alcohol.

"Aaron, it's going to fight me pulling it out, isn't it?" Pineda asked.

My eyes went large, realizing what she implied.

"I'm worried it'll cause so much damage your throat will start bleeding, it'll sever an artery or something on the way out," Pineda said. "Are there more limbs like the one I pulled?"

I nodded.

"Okay, we're going to anesthetize you, extract this...thing...through surgery," Pineda said.

I nodded again. What say did I have at this point?

"It's calmer now, right?" Pineda said.

I let my hand off, the creature squirmed down my throat—and into my stomach. I took the fullest breath I'd ever had in my life.

"What's going on?" Pineda asked.

"No choice now," I said.

"It moved down?" Pineda asked.

I nodded.

"I'm sorry, Aaron," she said.

"No, how could you know? I didn't," I said.

I felt small tinges all over my stomach, as if the scratched side of a Velcro strip clutched against the walls of my belly. No piercing stings, though. The limbs weren't flailing; I felt a heavy weight in my stomach.

"I think it settled. Feels like I ate Thanksgiving dinner. It's sticking to the inside walls of my stomach, feels like it's setting up camp," I said.

"Okay, we're going to move you into surgery. I'm going to call Doctor Maron while we're on the way," said Pineda.

The sharp sting of the creature's limb dug its way into my stomach. Groaning, reflux came up from my stomach. The acid in my throat; stinging flavor surged from my stomach to the base of my tongue. My chest spasmed.

"Talk to me, Aaron," Pineda said, unlocking the hospital bed as she spoke to me. The other nurses helped wheel the bed out of the room. Pineda pulled her cell phone out to call Maron.

"That claw you pulled out," I said. "It's got more, damned thing is digging in and digging in hard," I said.

"Using those pinchers to hold on?" she asked.

"More like nailing itself into place," I said.

The fluorescent lights in the ceiling passed by every few seconds. Once a light came closer, I focused on it, looking closer at the bulb so I could concentrate on something else. It didn't help. I felt each sharp end embed in the walls of my stomach.

"Hey, it's Pineda. Plan on anesthesia immediately upon arrival, it's moved into his stomach, causing severe pain," Pineda said.

A tear. One of the pinchers moved down, slicing the stomach. The pincher's edge moved further, it hadn't breached my stomach, but the organ was being cut open. My expulsive shout cut off as my voice crackled.

"Aaron?" Pineda said. She spoke into her cell quickly, "Maron, be ready, immediate surgery to remove this from his stomach."

Pineda put her phone away. I tried to respond, couldn't speak as my breathing pulsated without control. My back stretched; I took a strong intake of oxygen.

"Aaron, can you tell me what happened?" she asked.

"It cut my stomach open," I said.

"Okay, we're speeding up," Pineda ordered.

The fluorescent lights sped over me. The surgery room doors hummed as they opened. The pincher moved, ripping the hole in my stomach a little larger. I closed my eyes, wincing from the surge of pain in my stomach. I could feel my stomach slowly emptying, contents of its acid pumping out from the open wound.

"Fill me in," a doctor asked. I didn't recognize the voice, it wasn't Maron. I didn't open my eyes. I just tried to breathe.

"Esophageal foreign body. Moved and lodged into his stomach," Pineda responded.

"Why surgery then? Isn't the esophageal area clear?" the doctor asked.

"Yes, but it moved into his stomach and used its pinchers to lodge its way against the stomach walls. At least one tear," Pineda said. "Aaron, any more tears or just punctures elsewhere?"

"Think just one tear," I said.

"What do you mean 'it?'" the doctor asked.

"It's a bug. A creature of some sort," Pineda said. "Patient described the body feeling like a large tongue. It also has long, bug-like limbs. During one attempt for extraction, I pulled a limb off," Pineda said. "Here. Emilia, hand me the bag."

I looked over at the IV drip, desperate for anesthesia so I wouldn't feel a thing anymore. Nothing else mattered.

"The hell?" the doctor said, staring at the severed limb, sealed in plastic.

104

A different pincher sliced another hole. Like a sharpened knife, it lacerated my flesh.

"Oh, oh, oh," I said. "Another cut."

"All right, let's get anesthesia going," the doctor said. "We have to stop his stomach acid from eating his other organs."

"And..." Pineda said.

"No shit, we have to remove the organism, too," the doctor shouted.

The tongue was bigger. I felt its end moving toward the new cut. Its width slithered, feeling drastically larger.

"It's moving, moving toward the opening," I said. "The pinchers, they're all moving toward the cut," I said.

"Where? Can you point to it?" Pineda asked.

I pointed to the side of my abs, pointing without hesitation because I could feel exactly where the tongue and the pinchers moved toward.

"Doctor Cornett is our anesthesiologist, he'll be getting you to sleep and taken care of," Pineda said.

I nodded.

Doctor Cornett hovered over my head, putting a mask over my face. "Mr. Crowley. I normally have a longer routine than this, but I want to get you going, you know I'm putting you under to have surgery on your stomach?"

I nodded.

"Great, start counting down from ten," Doctor Cornett said.

"Ten," I said. "Nine."

I couldn't say eight. The tongue reached the hole. The pinchers moved to the edges of the tear and stretched out. My stomach ripped open and the pinchers moved forward, headed for my skin. My voice couldn't even scream.

The pinchers tore through my skin. My hand clutched Doctor Pineda's coat. Fingers grasping at the fabric.

My eyes went heavy. I couldn't discern whether it was the anesthesia, or my body going into shock. Everything became a blur. The gray walls a muddied shape; people in the room blurred figures moving about.

"What the hell is that?" Emilia shouted.

I heard a metal tray full of tools crash. As blood poured from my stomach, I felt the weight of the tongue portion of its body slide out of me, the pinchers clawing it forward. I tried to look. All I made out was a slithering mass supported by moving legs.

"What the hell is that?" Emilia shouted again.

"Kill it!" Pineda yelled.

More metal clanged.

"Maron, look out," Pineda said. "Maron!"

I heard a garbled scream.

"Cornett, where are you going?" Emilia asked.

A high-pitched roar followed the sound of pinchers sinking into flesh.

"Cornett!" Pineda shouted.

Pineda and Emilia shouted some more. My vision was nearly gone completely, I couldn't see a thing.

"Everyone out!" Pineda said. "Get Aaron."

"No, he could have more in him," Emilia shouted.

I was passing out. The muffled sounds of a struggle in the room were all I heard in my last moments of consciousness.

"Aaron. Aaron, I'm sorry. It's blocking me from getting to you. We have to quarantine this room to avoid it escaping," Pineda said. "I can't get you out."

The sound of people tripping over the metal pans and equipment as they evacuated echoed through the room.

"Police are on the way," Emilia said. "They may be able to get Aaron out."

The creature's pinchers hooked my ribs as it climbed onto my chest. I felt the weight of the body, the shape of a massive, slimy tongue, wriggling up my torso.

"Aaron," Pineda said. "I'm so sorry."

I nodded. The doors of the room slammed shut.

ALL YOURS

MELISSA KOONS

FEATURED IN "UNDERCURRENTS" RELEASED BY WORD FIRE PRESS

The storm raged against the ship. The wooden vessel creaked and groaned as the winds tossed its belly along the ferocious waves. Men shouted above, but their cries were drowned out by the screeching sleet that pounded the deck like stones. A gale blew against the ship, making the clipper pitch violently to the port side. It was a new vessel, the first of its kind having only been created two years prior in 1843, but the storm made the wooden ship groan as if it had seen a thousand voyages.

I hit the hull as my body was flung with the momentum of the ship's rocking. I heard a muffled shout up top before it was sharply cut off and then drowned out by the howling storm. Regaining my footing, I gathered my irons and pressed oakum between the planks, fitting the caulking fiber into any gaps to ensure the seal between the wood remained watertight.

"Beckett! Get yer arse o'er here! We got another leak," the boatswain, Ricky, shouted at me from across the hold.

I scrambled over the boxes of cargo and supplies, sliding across the slick floor. Water seeped through a crack in the hull. Ricky pressed his hands against the wood, trying—and failing—to plug the leak with his thin fingers. Grabbing a wooden plug from my tool kit, I hammered it into the leak. Water spurted as the plug sank deeper into the planks.

"Get some blankets from the forecastle! We need to pack them around the cargo. If the tea or opium gets wet you can say good-bye to ever eatin' again," Ricky shouted.

I dropped my tools and darted up the ladder to the galley. Just as I reached the forecastle, the ship rocked again, and then the violent pitching caused by the rough winds and turbulent ocean was suddenly over. Confused, I remained in the galley a moment, clutching the blankets in my arms, listening intently to the men shouting outside. The pounding sleet had lightened to a soft rain that pattered against the deck.

"Hey, Ricky, I think the storm's passing!" I shouted down to him. I expected to hear a gruff chuckle or a grunt of acknowledgment, but Ricky stayed silent.

Walking over to the ladder, I climbed down into the hold. "Ricky? Did ya hear me?" I asked, looking around the crates for the boatswain. I found him near the hull, hunched over with his ear pressed against the planks. "Ricky?" I asked, slowing my steps.

He looked up at me, his familiar unshakeable demeanor faltering slightly. His sun-weathered face blanched. "I think the storm was the least of our problems, kid," he said, his voice scratchy and hushed. He leaned closer to the hull and closed his eyes.

Overhead, I heard the pounding of the crew's boots stall for the briefest of moments.

"Captain! Starboard side!" the sailing master shouted.

"There, in the water!" another man shouted.

I looked to Ricky with a confused frown, but he just took a deep breath and kept his eyes closed. I mirrored Ricky and pressed my ear against the hull. I could hear splashing, but nothing seemed out of the ordinary considering the storm we'd just come through. But I was only fifteen, so I wasn't sure what was considered "ordinary" on the ship.

As soon as I came of age six months ago, I'd joined Captain Henderson's crew. We'd set out for China to get our cargo and made it there in ninety days. We expected the return journey to be about the same since our magnificent ship was one of the fastest clippers on the sea. We only had two weeks left to our journey before we would make port at home and claim our riches for the coveted teas and opium in our hold.

The crew's voices were muffled, but Ricky and I were still able to make out what the men up top were saying through the planks. "It-it can't be . . . it's just a legend . . ." the captain stammered.

"Ain't they good luck fer a sailor?" the sailing master asked.

"No," Ricky whispered beside me.

The ship pitched to the starboard side, and an inhuman growl echoed throughout the hold as something climbed on board the ship. Panicked, I started to run toward the ladder, but Ricky grabbed my wrist and pulled me back. I stared up through the tiny gaps in the wood at the shadows crossing overhead.

"Lower the lifeboat!" the captain shouted.

Men shouted commands back and forth, but they were soon drowned out by ferocious growls. Their frantic shouts turned to screams.

Ricky's eyes focused on the planks above us, following the sounds of the men as they scrambled up top. Another growl reverberated through the ship. The rapid beating of boots against the planks was halted by a sinister scraping of leather against wood. The crew's terrible screams permeated the air before they were abruptly cut off. A thick stream of blood poured through the cracks in the planks above us, and the thin rays of surface light that had seeped into the hold were now blocked by heavy, fallen shadows.

I opened my mouth to scream, to ask what to do, to plead to God, but Ricky slapped his hand across my lips and shook his head at me, urging me to stay silent. We listened as the few remaining sailors on deck tried to escape the creature that had boarded our vessel.

After the longest and shortest minutes of my life, everything fell silent. The heavy shadows above us jerked, and then were ripped away, showering us with blood. I startled, but remained silent. I listened to the crunching of bones and slurping of flesh as the creature devoured its meal.

Ricky let out a shuddering breath and closed his eyes. The main deck groaned as the creature slithered along the planks, dragging its engorged body across the ship, searching for any survivors. It seemed like an eternity before the ship swayed portside with the weight of the satiated creature. Ricky and I stumbled, reaching out to grab the hull to brace ourselves from falling and giving ourselves away. We held our breath and listened to the distinct splash as the creature returned to the depths of whatever hell it had emerged from.

After the creature hit the water, there were no other sounds except the lapping of waves against the ship and the caws of circling seagulls. Neither Ricky nor I spoke, we didn't move, and we barely breathed.

Ricky clapped his hand on my shoulder and covered his rough face with his other. The stream of blood had thinned to a drip above us, but it wasn't the only one. The entire ceiling seemed to be raining drops of blood into the cargo hold.

Following the drip lines, I noticed that our clothes were spotted with the horrific rain, the blood of our crew. My legs trembled. Ricky's hand on my shoulder tightened, holding me upright.

"No time fer that, kid," he said morosely. "Let's see if any of our men are still breathin',"

My head felt dizzy as I nodded in agreement. Ricky helped me regain my footing, and I followed closely behind him as we made our way up the ladder to the galley. Ricky paused. I wondered what he'd seen, and debated ducking back down into the protection of the hold. As if he knew my thoughts to flee, Ricky completed his climb and reached a hand down to help pull me up. As soon as my head poked over the edge of the hatch I saw the cause of Ricky's hesitation.

A severed arm stretched through the door, reaching toward the galley. There was no way to tell whom the arm belonged to, and I wasn't sure it mattered. A trail of smeared blood led through the forecastle and out onto the main deck. My stomach churned. I heaved and vomited onto the floor, my muscles clenching and nearly lifting me out of my skin with the force of it.

Ricky patted me on the back and closed his eyes. "It's okay, kid. It's ov'r," he grunted.

Despite the attempt to calm me, I could hear the lie in his words. The tension of his shoulders and the sadness in his voice told me he didn't believe it was over at all. Whatever had done this to our crew—the monster that devoured them and made strong men scream—wasn't far off.

Stepping over the severed arm, Ricky peeked around the corner. Identifying that everything was clear, he jerked his head, signaling for me to follow him.

I took a deep breath, swallowing down the rest of my dry heaves. I straightened and pulled myself together. I wasn't sure what Ricky was planning, but I knew I couldn't be a heaving mess in the galley if we were going to get through this. I followed his steps beyond the arm delicately, trying not to slip in the slimy blood congealed around the appendage.

Ricky led the way through the forecastle, stopping short when he reached the main deck. "Ha'e mercy," he breathed out, his eyes wide while he scanned the carnage. The men— our men, our shipmates, our friends—were all gone. Well, not exactly *all* of them. Like the arm in the galley, there were fragments of the sailors scattered across the deck.

I closed my eyes and put all my strength into steadying my legs so I could move forward. Their remains told a story more horrifying than what I'd imagined. The deck was marred with scratch marks from the men clutching anything they could to avoid whatever terror devoured them. A pair of boots stood near the lifeboat—partially lowered at an awkward angle—with the owner's feet still inside them. The wooden planks were stained a rust color, the blood that had drenched them was drying and soaking deep into the woodgrain.

"Captain," Ricky whispered, walking toward the steering wheel. A fisted hand was wrapped around the spokes of the navigation wheel, a familiar tattoo on the severed wrist. Ricky's shoulders slumped, and he shook his head. "He was a good man."

I nodded. I'd spent five months with the captain and the crew. He had been a good man. They all had been.

"It never gets easier," Ricky muttered.

"What doesn't?" I asked, sidestepping a chunk of someone that oozed near the railing. I cringed and looked toward Ricky.

"Losin' good men. I've lost crews like this before," he said, staring off into the calm waves that stretched before us. "I had no choice."

"No choice?" A shiver crawled up my spine and made the hairs on my neck stand on end. I backed away from the railing, my eyes scanning the ocean waves for the beast that had devastated our ship. There was no disturbance in the sparkling depths, but a tension started to build in my chest that I couldn't shake.

"I thought I was dead. There had been a storm—jus' like this one—decades ago. It nearly ripped our ship apart, the sails split from the ice and the wind. We were gonners. Just when we all thought we were goin' down, it cleared." Ricky's shoulders slumped, and he held a spoke of the navigation wheel absentmindedly.

Listening to his story, I paced the main deck. The unsettling feeling in my chest tightened, but I couldn't explain why. The ocean was calm, and the skies were now clear. The seagulls circled overhead, their familiar caws echoing in the wisps of clouds. Such perfect conditions should have been a sailor's delight—but I was still on edge.

"I was in the sail locker gettin' a fresh sail when it came. I heard the growl—it shook the walls it was so loud."

The seagulls. Why were they just circling?

"My crew—I heard them scream. I heard them die. It wasn't a battle. There was no fight."

I looked at all the fresh meat around me and then back to the circling seagulls. Not one was making a dive for the deck. Not one seemed eager to fill its carrion gullet with the remains of the men. That could only mean the predator was still near. It hadn't finished its meal, yet.

"It was a feast," Ricky said, turning toward me. His brow was furrowed and his face drawn in anger. "I heard it all from the sail locker where I hid—like a coward. When their screams no longer echoed in my head, I came up top. It was . . . this," he said, gesturing to the aftermath of the gruesome slaughter.

I heard a splash off the portside, and my fear spiked. I reached for the nearest weapon—a paddle that had fallen out of the dangling lifeboat.

"I saw it. The creature that ate 'em. I stared into its eyes as it filled its belly with my crew."

The splashing got closer, lapping at the hull below me. I crouched, readying myself for the monster to rear its head. I held the paddle out in front of me, unsure how to use it in battle but determined to fight the creature off.

"That's when she saved me. A beauty too good ter be true. She helped me reach port, helped me collect the pay for all my fallen crew," Ricky said, his anger fading into sadness.

The muscles in my back were so taut they hurt. I softened my battle stance. The splashing continued below at the water's edge, but nothing boarded the ship.

"I had to repay her for her kindness. Twenty years, I've been workin' my contract with her. She always saves me," he mumbled, releasing his hold on the navigation wheel and walking toward the railing on the port side. He looked down at the blue waters, and a soft smile curled his lips.

Frowning, I took a cautious step forward. Ricky leaned against the railing, relaxed and at ease. Still armed with the paddle, I peeked over the edge, and my breath caught in my throat.

I stared down at the most beautiful creature I'd ever seen. Her hair shimmered like starlight in the afternoon sun, and her alabaster skin had an unearthly glow to it. She turned her crystal green eyes away from Ricky and looked at me. My heart hammered in my chest, and I was filled with a sensation I couldn't name. She smiled at me—the sweetest smile I'd ever seen on a woman's face. I sighed, the dread melting away and replaced with a burning warmth that comforted me. I could see all my dreams in her eyes, and all my fears vanished on her voiceless, supple lips.

I dropped my weapon. I watched her splash in the waves, swimming carelessly with an air of delight and peace. "What is she?" I asked.

"Don't you know the legends, kid?" Ricky sneered. "She's a bloody mermaid."

I couldn't hear the seagulls above me anymore, but I didn't care. "I didn't think they were real," I said, unable to break my eyes away from hers.

"Aye, they are," Ricky said, the sadness returning to his voice. "Let me keep this one, please," he begged her. The mermaid turned her gaze away from mine and gave Ricky a charming smile. "He's just a boy," he said, shaking his head.

I blinked, my senses slowly returning to me. I looked toward the skies. The seagulls had flown away; I could spot their beating wings in the distance, but the breeze did not carry their familiar cries back to me. I looked down at the deck still untouched by their greedy beaks.

"Haven't you had yer fill?" Ricky asked, his tone sharp and biting.

The calmness that had settled within me trickled away as the tightness of dread and fear coiled within my breast. I backed away from the railing, my eyes locked on to Ricky's hunched shoulders. It wasn't relaxation that had softened his posture—it was defeat.

"You—you said she saved you?" I said, tripping backward and sprawling on the blood-soaked planks.

Ricky turned toward me, sadness in his eyes. "She did," he said. He walked toward me, his boots falling heavily on the wood. Each reverberation made my heart pound faster. Tears leaked from my eyes, and I scooted back, ignoring that my hands squished in the entrails of my friends.

"You said she saved you!" I shouted.

Ricky nodded, overcoming my weak escape in several strides. "She did save me." He scooped me up by my collar and dragged me back toward the railing.

I thrashed against him, clawing at his wrist. "H-how will you bring the ship to port? You can't do it by yourself." I wiggled out of his grasp and rolled away from him. "I-I can help! I'll help!" I bargained.

He paused, his eyes focused on the water beyond the railing. "It would be easier with two," he whispered.

I nodded, but he wasn't addressing me. There was a silent battle being waged, and my fate hung in the balance. I held my breath, waiting for the sword to slice and seal my life one way or the other.

Ricky shook his head. He stormed toward me, fisting his hand around my throat, stealing the breath from me.

Choking, I tried to yank his hand away, but he heaved me across the deck, tossing me at the base of the railing.

My heart plummeted, and I whimpered, shaking my head. "Please, no," I croaked. I tried to dart away from him again, but he was faster than me and caught me mid-lunge.

"Sorry, kid." He muttered, hoisting me over the railing.

I reached out, trying to grab hold of him, the railing—anything—but everything slipped through my fingers. Despair choked me as I hit the waters. Opening my eyes, I could see the sunlight twinkling above me, and the darkness of the deep ocean gaping below me. I turned, and there she was in all her splendor. Her perceived beauty from where I had stood on the ship turned to horror as I swam beneath the rippling surface.

Her piercing green eyes glowed in the blue currents, her pupils becoming vertical slits like a shark's. Her alabaster skin was luminescent, and the gills in her throat and ribs gaped with each breath she took. Her fin whipped through the waters like a blade, and her webbed hands stretched toward me.

I jerked, trying to get away, but the ship was behind me, she was before me, and darkness loomed below me. There was no escape.

I looked up, seeing Ricky's distorted figure watching from the deck. I tried to swim to the surface, but her cold hand was on my cheek before I could breach. I couldn't comprehend how she moved through the water without disrupting the currents. Her nails dug into my temple, tearing the skin and making me scream in pain as she yanked me back down into the watery depths.

Air bubbles escaped my lips, and my lungs burned from lack of oxygen. She smiled—the most terrifying grin I'd ever seen. Her lips stretched back and revealed three rows of fang-like teeth. I closed my eyes. I didn't want her face to be the last thing I saw. My body shook, desperate for air. I tried to take in a gulp of water—wanting to drown before she ripped me apart with her fangs. I opened my mouth, ready for the rush of salt water and the blackness that would overtake me.

But it never came.

Her lips latched over mine, and oxygen flooded my lungs. She breathed air back into me, her nails digging into my throat to keep me anchored. I opened my eyes and was frozen by the lidless, green crystalline orbs that bore into my soul. Just when my lungs felt like they would burst, she let go.

A rope dropped into the water above my head. I grabbed it without hesitation. Ricky pulled me up the side of the ship. I hit the deck, gasping and sputtering seawater onto the wood. My body shook with shock, and my arms collapsed beneath my weight when I tried to push myself up.

"Take it easy there, kid," Ricky grunted, scooping me up under my arms and propping me against the railing.

"I-I don't understand," I gasped. I winced at the pain that shot through me and felt the tender, split skin of my throat.

"Twenty years is a long time, kid. Be thankful to her, it makes it easier," Ricky said, giving me a soft smile.

"Easier?" I choked out.

"To feed her, and repay yer debt." Ricky stood up from his crouch beside me, his face serious. His eyes held such pain in them tears trickled down his cheeks. He turned so his back was against the railing and spread out his arms. "All yours, sweetheart."

He flung himself backward, face toward the clear sky and a grin on his lips.

I choked on a sob as an inhuman growl filled the air.

He screamed once, and then it was silent.

I lay against the railing, the ship drifting along the current toward port. I didn't have to look to know she was still there. I could hear her splashing alongside the ship. When the afternoon sun met the horizon, I finally found the strength to push myself up. I shuffled my way to the navigation wheel, peering over the bow to the rolling waves.

Her sparkling head was unmistakable. Unclasping the captain's severed hand, I rolled the wheel in the direction she was swimming. "Alright, sweetheart. Take me home."

"Mermaids do that?" the incredulous young man in front of me gasped. His face was twisted in horror, and his head jerked from side to side, checking the waters around us for the terrifying creature. "*She* did *this*?"

I nodded. "She saved me, and I've been indebted to her—and Ricky—for the past fifteen years. It is my gift—and my curse," I said, looking up at the clear night sky. The full moon illuminated the glistening deck drenched in the blood of good men. A familiar splashing drew our attention to the starboard side, and a sad smile spread across my lips.

"No, no. You can't. I survived! You can't let her take me!" the young man shouted, backing away from me.

"Sorry, Willy. She only saves one." I grabbed him by his collar and flung him over the railing.

"All yours, sweetheart," I whispered, turning away.

His scream echoed in the crisp air long after it had been cut off, disturbing the stillness of the night.

GERMLINE ENHANCEMENT
THOMAS A. FOWLER

Within the labs of Touchpoint Genetics, Morgan readied an injector. Staring through the microscope, she watched the modified human eggs, ensuring she had viable embryos for implantation. Silver cabinets were all around the room, some expensive installations to cool vital components, others for storage of basic tools. The lights were designed to replicate natural sunlight, which couldn't enter the lab for fear of altering specimens.

"If you do this, we'll blur a line civilization has yet to cross," Yamamoto said.

"I know," Morgan replied. "It's one that will inevitably be crossed. Better us than anyone else. At least this will give Liv's children a chance."

Morgan's hair was gone. The scarf wrapped over her head had a patch sewed on of two robots holding hands. Her cheekbones prominently stuck out. Her brown eyes were hard to focus on from her bloodshot sclera.

"Your intent is good, but it opens doors to others without morals like yours," Yamamoto said.

"It opens the door to disease-less children, it opens the door to humans who don't suffer," Morgan replied. "Then animals that don't spread infection. Endangered species not falling prey to inherited, chronic defects."

"But where does it end?" Yamamoto asked.

Morgan marked one egg. Its cytoplasm just the right thickness. The corona radiata was perfect to supply vital proteins. She would use multiple eggs, but that one egg was it. This was the cell that would change evolutionary history.

"It ends when we have built a thriving species that guides a perfectly balanced planet," Morgan said. "One where you don't have to inject poison to eradicate unwanted cells."

"When does it stop, though?" Yamamoto said. "Do we have to modify disease? Why not dwarfism? Deafness?"

"People who are deaf don't consider themselves in need of a cure," Morgan said. "They are able to adapt."

"Parents choosing their embryos or modifying their sperm and eggs can decide whether it is." Yamamoto continued, "Society's treatment of people can determine it's something to be cured through germline enhancement."

"This is just for cancer," Morgan said.

"For now," Yamamoto said. "Then what? The process can be replicated to remove anything."

"We're not even sure this will work," Morgan replied.

"But if it does, then any geneticist will have the keys to altering future generations," Yamamoto said.

Morgan pulled the eggs, readying them for invitro fertilization. "Then it will be up to scientists to practice responsibly and have the conversation."

"Aren't we doing that? And once the technology is available it won't be up to scientists. We're in a privately funded lab. They have access to all of your research. If they can sell it, they will. Profits will be astronomical because countries will pay anything to get ahead of this. Entire ethnicities could disappear over enough time if they don't pay."

"You and I could be the geneticists capable of eradicating cancer," Morgan said.

She coughed. Blood trickled from her mouth.

"This pain could be removed from the human experience," Morgan said.

"Then let's continue the somatic research. Let's cure the individual because then it's a choice, it's a singular treatment," Yamamoto said. "We have nearly extracted and removed all cancerous cells through somatic therapy. If we took your process and applied it, then we've cured cancer, Morgan."

"That Touchpoint will see at an overpriced margin accessible only to the rich," Morgan said.

"What? Do you think germline enhancement will be made free? Available to low income families or impoverished countries? Touchpoint will profit no matter what we do," Yamamoto said. "So let's take the route that lets humanity respond to how it wants to be individually, not give those in power the ability to make humans who they think we should become."

"Let's get the mother," Morgan said.

"No," Yamamoto said. "We know the genetic trait that makes cancer more likely. Let this mother give birth to her children, then we give somatic therapy to proactively treat the child so they have a chance but we don't open the floodgates to a master race."

"Please, we won't implement a master race," Morgan said.

"How do you know?" Yamamoto asked. "How do you know someone won't gain access to influencing how kids look, act, and respond for future generations, then make sure others who don't adhere are eliminated? It's impossible."

"I have no time left on this earth," Morgan said. "My chance to leave a legacy is here, in this room."

"I know. You could be the person who helped a mother with cancer have children, then upon their birth treat them to avoid cancer, like an immunization. Or you could be the geneticist who decided humans should be able to decide their evolutionary future, which will end with someone taking advantage of that. You cannot entrust humanity with this level of responsibility."

Morgan opened the door to the lab. Inside the waiting room, Liv anxiously tapped her feet, reading on her smartphone. Fingers tapped the case in a nervous rhythm.

"Ms. Brooks, come on in," Morgan said. "Do you prefer Ms. Brooks or Liv?"

"Liv, please," she replied.

"Dr. Morgan, our conversation wasn't over," Yamamoto said. "I feel it warrants more."

"And I feel that, as my lab assistant, you assist me in my research," Morgan said. She turned her attention to Liv. "How long have you been in remission?"

"Three months, officially, last Thursday," Liv said.

"That's amazing," Morgan said. "I haven't experienced remission yet. It's a large reason I wanted you to come down here, so I can finish my work before I'm in hospital for the foreseeable future."

"Dr. Morgan," Yamamoto said.

"Yes, Dr. Yamamoto?" she replied.

"Can I speak with you for just a moment?"

"Yes. Liv, go ahead and get comfortable on the table there," Morgan said.

They walked over to the storage unit.

"Save the germline research, let me continue your work to modify it for somatic therapy. That way Liv can have children without a fear of passing cancerous genetic traits, but it remains a responsive therapy. You eradicate the problem, without adjusting the genetic composition of future generations. The impact, of which, has influences you and I cannot predict what it will do to humanity or even potentially evolution."

"You traveled here on a grant from your country where germline research is banned, correct?" Morgan asked.

"Yes, but I didn't come for that reason," Yamamoto said.

"Yet, you still came to the frontier where germline research has guidelines, but is allowed," Morgan said. "You can't enter the Wild West and expect to not get your hands dirty."

"I think it has, but we could make the West worse than we could ever anticipate," Yamamoto said. "Evolution and mother nature have ways of keeping us in balance."

"As lead on this laboratory, your services are no longer needed," Morgan said. "This experiment has been authorized, is within genetic guidelines, and I'm going to perform this procedure before I'm in a hospital bed, fed through a tube, and counting the hours until the cancer takes me and the pain finally stops. Thank you for everything you've done, Dr. Yamamoto."

Morgan extended her hand. Yamamoto's eyes were wide in fear. She stepped back slowly, not letting Morgan out of her sight. She didn't shake Morgan's hand.

"You're going to change humanity itself," Yamamoto said. "Liv, I can help your children once they're born, we don't have to change your eggs, we don't have to change who we are."

"That's enough," Morgan said. She ushered Yamamoto out of the room. Paging security, she whispered into the telecom. "Security, Dr. Yamamoto is no longer on my project, please see that she does not enter my lab, especially while our procedure is ongoing."

Yamamoto knew there was nothing to be done at this point. Touchpoint wouldn't risk losing so much on a previously authorized procedure. Too much investment upfront. Looking through the observatory glass, she walked calmly out from the hallway. "Please don't," she whispered, inaudibly, one last time, hoping that Morgan would listen.

"She seems to want to try something else?" Liv said.

"Yes, difference of opinion. Not much different from the news coverage we discussed that's going on right now about your procedure," Morgan said.

"I understand," Liv said. "You and the doctors explained it in quite a bit of detail."

"Then let's get started," said Morgan.

"So what happens after today?" Liv asked.

"We wait to find out if the path to eradicating cancer has been made through you," Morgan answered.

Dr. Morgan rested in her hospital bed, waiting for death. It had been weeks since she was hospitalized and her pain intensified with each day as the cancer consumed her. She repeatedly tapped the button for her morphine drip. It had been a while and another release would be allowed in a few minutes. She tapped, waiting for the beep to indicate another morphine drip starting.

Outside her room, nurses and doctors worked on unusual plans, Morgan eavesdropped.

"We can move these patients into rooms 24 and 27. That'd clear up the South Hall, then we make sure we isolate the hall and keep our area from any cross-contamination," a nurse said.

"Think that's the best we can do," a doctor replied. "Wait, we have those two patients incoming."

"Double up on low-level treatment? We have dividers if we need them," the nurse suggested.

"Okay, sure they'll understand once they hear the circumstances. As you do your rounds ask if we have any volunteers for doubling up," another doctor said. "Let's not…"

The doctor lowered his voice. Morgan couldn't make anything out. Until she heard "room 18." Then he spoke normally again. "I just don't think it'll be a yes."

"Agreed," a nurse said.

Morgan knew who they were talking about, the guy named Clark. She'd never met him, but room 18 tended to be a rowdy one. Clark shouted a lot. She'd even heard a bedpan get thrown at few days ago. He hadn't taken to terminal cancer or accepted how to die peacefully.

"Okay, let's get maintenance up here to start work on extra installations; in the meantime, let's all follow protocol and make sure we're ready for this," the doctor said. "Few of our patients can afford to fight an infection like this one."

Once they dispersed, Morgan felt the pain rise within her body again, the exhaustive wear of cancer. When the morphine drip still wouldn't beep, she knew her timing was off. It may be a while still before the pain medication would be allowed to go into her IV again through the automated system. Rather than focus on the pain, she turned on the television in the hospital room.

Swapping between daytime soap operas and bad reality tv, nothing of interest came up. She resorted to the news. The political news continued the ongoing divide, pointing fingers for problems they both had hands in causing, and debated without end.

Morgan looked out at the hallway, seeing everyone move with a purpose. She wanted the nurse to come in, that way Morgan could ask what was going on. Clearly, they needed extra beds, but obviously not for cancer treatment or the like. The need for separation meant there could've been some sort of outbreak. It wasn't far from flu season. Morgan wondered if this year's strain had become particularly troublesome.

"Turning to local news, an outbreak of a troubling illness has residents concerned," the newscaster said. "We'll have more on, and tips for how to keep your family safe, after the break."

Nurse Debney knocked on the door. "Hey, Dr. Morgan."

Morgan waved.

"How are you feeling today?" Debney asked.

Morgan shrugged. "Same old, same old. What's going on out there?"

"Oh, nasty infection of sorts going around," Debney replied.

"It was only a matter of time before the antigenic drift found a way to overcome our vaccines," Morgan said.

Debney paused, taken aback by her knowledge of the terminology. "What'd you do before you came here?"

"I was a geneticist," Morgan replied.

"Ah, I was wondering," Debney said. "You should tell me more things about yourself, fact that you've been here as long as you have, I don't think I could tell you much about your life."

"Doesn't matter, not much life left to know about anyways," Morgan replied.

"I don't like talk like that." Debney continued, "My opinion, and this is coming from someone who's seen a lot of folks come and go, the last weeks can be what matter the most, because it's the last impression people have of you."

"That's the hope," Morgan said.

"For?" Debney asked.

"For leaving an impression, leaving a legacy behind of what you've accomplished. What you've done," Morgan said.

The news came back from commercial. Morgan didn't listen. Debney worked on getting vitals. Morgan pressed the IV drip button, a beep. Morgan sighed calmly, knowing the morphine would come in moments as it worked its way into her saline mixture.

The intercom beeped. "Rapid Response Team. Emergency Center. Room 12." Another beep. "Rapid Response Team. Emergency Center. Room 12."

"Never like hearing that," Debney said.

The intercom beeped again. "Code Gray. Emergency Center. Room 12."

Debney and Morgan looked at one other, confused.

"Now, how's your pain level?" Debney asked.

"It's fine after the drip starts, but it's getting pretty intense by the time the cycle becomes available again," Morgan said.

"Okay, that happens. We've had the same drip for a few days and we're within range to increase the dosage slightly. I'll put a note in to Doctor Taylor to get that authorized," Debney said.

The intercom beeped again. "Code Gray. Triage. Room 3."

"What the hell's going on down there?" Debney asked.

The intercom beeped. "Security Alert. Aggressive, violent female. Maternity Hall."

"Jesus," Morgan said. "What's going on out there?"

"Yeah, I'll be right back, going to see what's going on," Debney said. "You stay put."

"Hard to go anywhere, for multiple reasons," Morgan replied.

Debney left the room. She looked around for a colleague.

"Hey, John, what's going on?" Debney asked.

John, a fellow nurse, walked with her as he headed for the hall entrance. "Multiple patients are acting up that have this infection. Not sure, starts with tetany cramps, causes extreme muscular contractions."

This time, the intercom didn't beep, there was no automated alert. This was a person hopping on the speaker system live. "Attention: All Personnel. Code Silver. No weapons. Aggressive patients. Repeat: Code Silver."

"Okay, that's a lockdown. Nurses, lights out in rooms," Debney took charge. "Med Techs, seal all doors."

Debney entered Morgan's room, turned off the lights and closed the door. Outside of the room, a massive crash sounded—like a door being busted open. A few screams came from the room down the hall.

"Ma'am, please calm down," a male shouted. "God!" The man's plea turned to a scream. Another massive crash.

Debney put up the privacy curtain and hunkered down beside Morgan's hospital bed. As the two remained still, they could hear someone coming closer.

"What room?" a voice gargled. It sounded familiar to Morgan, but she couldn't quite pinpoint it.

"Here, on the left," another, familiar, voice replied.

Someone pulled on the door handle, trying to get through the lock. Then the door to Morgan's room burst open. Morgan and Debney remained still. The privacy curtain pulled back.

Liv entered the room. Her body completely different. The definition of her muscles looked like a bodybuilder, each muscle fiber individually strained and swollen. Veins popped in clear separation from the contracting muscle structure. Sweat dripped down her brow in heavy, consistent drops.

"Liv?" Morgan said.

Liv looked down at Debney. "You have one chance to leave."

Debney stood. "Now, Dr. Morgan is a patient of mine, it's my responsibility to keep her safe."

"Well, I was one of hers," Liv said. "She did this to me."

The intercom beeped again. "Code Gray. Main Lobby, Emergency Center and Triage."

"She's also the reason for all your emergency codes. She did this to those people down there," Liv said.

Debney didn't move. She didn't say anything, just breathed as the situation played out.

"Did she tell you what she did before having to stay here?" Liv asked.

Debney couldn't muster a response. Outside the room, everyone evacuated. The scattering people hurried out, desperate to leave the cancer ward to a safer place.

"Did she?" Liv asked. Her veins gave off a strange ebb, changing in shape as a rippling effect came from her body.

Debney confirmed, shaking her head.

"What was it?" Liv asked.

"Geneticist," Debney replied.

"Exactly, and in an effort to get rid of the cancer killing her, she told me she could alter my baby's genetics with germline...what'd you call it?" Liv asked.

"Germline enhancement, resulting in your future generations not being adverse to cancer," Morgan replied.

"Didn't work, though?" Liv put gloves on her hands, then grabbed Morgan. "My eggs didn't make it. And because of the changes your tests did to me...now I'm the host."

"The host of what?" Morgan asked.

The intercom beeped. "Due to increased security threats, remain where you are. Police assistance is on the way."

"That," Liv replied.

"What?" Morgan asked.

"You made her germline enhancement a spreadable reaction." Yamamoto stepped into the room, a computer balanced in her hands. "By trying to alter future generations, you found the way to genetically transmit it easily to others."

The news showed spreading chaos within the area. People weren't being torn apart. They were being infected; given the germline enhancement to become one of them.

"I want you to watch the news, hear what's happening. I want you to witness," Liv said. "Initially people will panic, but in time they'll see this transition is nothing violent. A simple touch is all it takes."

"And then what? You'll kill me?" Morgan asked.

"God no, I've been genetically altered; I haven't become a monster. You made me stronger, smarter. Now I can get the rest of society on board, and we'll be the better race," Liv said.

More altered humans gathered in the room. They looked at Morgan with curiosity. Almost like they wondered if they gained a glimpse of their creator.

"We are all capable of communicating as one, working as a race toward the betterment of one another. It was almost instantaneous. I accidentally touched my barista's hand and suddenly, we could speak to each other on another plane. We realized we had a way to unify the species. We have you to thank. You, Dr. Morgan," Liv said. "Dr. Yamamoto, if you please."

Yamamoto uploaded files to her computer. She loaded them onto a cloud-based drive. As she did, Liv pulled up her smartphone. Streaming live, she showed the computer and her muscular definition.

"Right now, many people in my area are being converted. Converted to a genetically superior version of humanity. I did this because I was promised a child by this doctor. That child did not arrive." Liv pointed the camera at

132

Morgan's face. "That child was taken from me. Now, you will all become my children. Children of a better race. Geneticists, you'll find the plans for germline enhancement that made me superior on the cloud. It's free to take. I recommend conversion now. We can all communicate as a single race telepathically, meaning we work as a collective whole, far superior to human kind."

"When you said 'unify the species,' you weren't talking about homo sapiens," Morgan said.

"No, humans are fallible, our species will be its replacement," Liv replied.

Yamamoto held up the laptop, letting Liv show the file location to the world.

"What are you doing?" Morgan asked.

"Expediting the inevitable," Yamamoto said. "Overcoming this city will take only a few weeks, Morgan. The spread will be exponential. The genetic power is too strong and too easily passed to human hosts."

Morgan stared at Yamamoto, struggling to understand. "Why?"

"Because you made the decision for us, I'm simply embracing it now that it's been made." She lifted the sleeve of her shirt. Her forearm muscles defined, veins rising. The fibers of her muscles tightened and worked their way toward her shoulder.

Liv finished her video stream. "We want this to be a peaceful transition, and I look forward to providing you with the peace I now feel."

Putting her smartphone away, Liv turned toward Dr. Morgan.

"You could convert me," Morgan said. "It could beat my cancer."

"Why do you think I haven't touched you," Liv replied. "Why do you think I put on these gloves? You'll live out the

133

rest of your cancer as punishment for never giving me my child. Punishment for taking the risk of altering my body. Punishment for not speaking up when you know there was a bigger risk, when Yamamoto warned you of what could happen. Punishment so you can watch as the conversion continues, but not participate."

"I was worried you'd get a God complex from your actions," Yamamoto said. "Because you played God and altered our species, I won't let you live to be worshipped. You'll die along with your research. That way this transformation will happen, and no one will be able to recreate it to do this ever again. We'll become the superior species and keep a balance humanity never could."

Liv and Yamamoto walked to the door.

A man joined them in the doorway, flexing his muscles and observing the veins that bulged on his skin.

"Clark," Debney whispered in astonishment. "You're— you're..."

"Evolved," Clark stepped back so that Liv and Yamamoto could exit. "Healed."

Liv paused at the door frame, turned back and smiled at Morgan. "Congratulations, Dr. Morgan. You have your lasting legacy before death. You've eradicated homo sapiens."

RECONCILING THE DRAGON
MELISSA KOONS
FEATURED IN "DRAGON WRITERS" RELEASED BY WORD FIRE PRESS

To: The Doctor with the Glasses

It's been four weeks since I left your camp. When I stumbled my way out of the darkness that night, I had no idea what you had done to me. What months of being closed up in your camp was intended to do to a person. It took a period of adjustment, and I know you are out there seeking me, but I'm reconciling myself and you'll never find us. Not yet. In the meantime, until I see you again, you will be glad to know that I have taken to many coffee shops and public gatherings to learn more about my reconciliation that you have put me on the track toward. It's strange being in these places; there is so much light compared to the places I used to call home.

This reconciliation isn't what I expected. Hell, I had no idea what to expect, but I didn't expect this. I knew there was a Dragon within me: angry, volatile, and filled with greed. You brought that Dragon out. Your devices, as horrible as they were, succeeded. I saw his glowing scales as his golden

135

eyes flared ominously into mine. He has the power to destroy, and that is all he wanted to do. That is all he had been allowed to do. I had been afraid that he would kill me: open his jaw and swallow me whole until there was no trace of me left. What had existed of me, I feared, would disappear without a trace, without memorial, without even a whisper on the wind. I would simply vanish, and all that would remain was this Dragon. That's when I ran. When you had pulled him out of me and I stared into those hateful eyes, I couldn't bear to be in the same room as him. I didn't want him. I didn't want to claim him, and I couldn't bear the thought of him consuming me so I did what any clinically sane person should do: fled. I had heard the search party you sent after me. I saw the bouncing light from the torches you carried. But he was still there, that Dragon. He was breathing down my neck at every turn. I couldn't escape those flaming eyes or those teeth.

It was only when I accepted that there was no running from him that I could begin the reconciliation process. That's why I like frequenting these coffee shops. I had never noticed before—never been driven to sit and actually look at the world and people surrounding me—but coffee shops really are the perfect place to see the world as it truly is. Every one of these people here has a Dragon. I have yet to see one as angry as mine, but then again, those Dragons don't typically like coffee; they need something much stronger to quell them. I haven't returned to those places seeking to quell my Dragon although it wants to.

The woman by the door has a blue one. She sits at the same table every Saturday afternoon with a book and a pen, sipping on hot tea because coffee is too bitter. Her Dragon is docile, and rests its head on her shoulder while she reads. Before you pulled my Dragon out of me, I never would have noticed the air of loneliness about her. Her Dragon sucks the heat from the air and makes the girl shiver in her self-inflicted isolation. I don't have the expertise and training that you do, Doctor, so I have no answers for her. I can only wonder what made her want to keep the world at arm's length, while her heart continues to yearn for connection. It's sad, really. She's only in her late-twenties or early-thirties. She still has so many possibilities available to her, but her Dragon keeps her tethered to this emptiness.

The boy with the red hair at the booth by the counter, he has a black one. He is talking to a girl around his age—they both look like they are right out of high school— her Dragon is pink and frightened of the boy with the red hair, but she talks to him anyway. I've never seen him here before, but I can see why the young girl's Dragon fears him. She fidgets in her seat, shifting her weight and shuffling her feet. She toys with a locket she wears around her neck, twisting it this way and that on the silver chain. Her Dragon urges her to leave, pokes at her, makes her itch, but the desperation the girl feels for a false realty that was promised to her makes her silent the Dragon.

If you were here I know you'd help the poor girl. You'd see the way the boy with the red hair's black Dragon looks at her and it would make you squirm. You'd know just what to say, Doctor. You'd smile politely, and pull the girl away while making everyone around you think the world was a perfect place. As I watch the young couple's interactions I am torn. The heat from my Dragon's breath burns my neck and I know what course of action it wants to take. Before I can decide whether or not it would be wise to unleash the destructive force within me, they leave.

I'm pretty sure I won't see that girl again.

Talk to you soon, Doctor.

Me

To: The Doctor with the Glasses

I passed a man on the way to the subway today. He seemed average enough, nothing special about him that caught my eye, but something in his scent called out my Dragon and made it snarl. You should have seen the terror in the man's eyes as he stared my Dragon down. His legs quivered and my Dragon engulfed him in flames. I felt powerless as I watched the exchange. I wanted to stop the Dragon, to pull him back, but there was nothing I could do. I still fear he will turn on me one of these days and devour me if I'm not careful. Maintaining this reconciliation with my Dragon is not as easy as I had hoped it would be. Then again, you never promised me easy. I wonder, from time to time, if I had stayed at the camp with you would it still be this difficult? The man from the subway ran away from me. I can't blame him. I ran away from the Dragon, too. I felt horrible after the exchange with the man. The whole ride on the train to my stop, I pondered why the Dragon felt it necessary to attack him. What drew the Dragon out? I thought I had gotten a handle on it, had learned to keep the Dragon in check, but obviously I was wrong. It seems I am not entirely in control—the Dragon will not follow my commands blindly—but I am not at its complete disposal, either. Since you'd brought him out, my usual process for coping with him no longer works. Now it is a strange kind of power struggle between my Dragon and me, but we are learning. He was so accustomed to devastation and I to repression, but our status quo has been upset and neither of us know where to go from here.

When I got to my coffee shop, I took my usual seat against the wall and nodded a hello to the woman with the blue dragon. I sat there maybe an hour, watching people come and go before I had my answer. The man in the subway was nothing special: he wore a suit that came off the rack and was untailored; he held a coffee in one hand and a briefcase in the other—nothing that would make anyone stop and think twice. The only thing slightly remarkable about him was his hair: a bright red that seemed far too familiar.

It's been two weeks since I've seen the boy with the red hair and his girl with the silver locket. I had had an uneasy feeling from the start, and when I saw her face on the news I wished I had let my Dragon out to do with the boy whatever it had wanted to do on that day. She's been missing for three days now, which I suppose is better than some alternatives. If only she had listened to her Dragon, if only she had acknowledged its existence maybe then she'd be safe.

I look around at all the people who come and go and it astounds me how many of us live our whole lives in denial of that single presence. We were taught as children to believe in magic, to play pretend and create entire worlds of fantasy. Somewhere along the line that was beaten out of us. It was as if imagination was only encouraged, nurtured, and accepted until the age of ten. Then, we were beaten constantly—steadily— with heavy tools to make us better, to make us wiser. We were beaten with logic and reason, responsibility and obligation, expectation and convention, until we no longer believed that dragons were ever real.

If it wasn't for you, Doctor, my Dragon would have consumed me long ago without my ever knowing it was there. I repressed him with toxins, ignoring his presence, until he would have devoured me. My fears of vanishing would have come true and, unlike the girl with the silver locket, no one would have ever known I was gone. Now I know, Dragons are very real and they live within us all whether we acknowledge them or not. Not all Dragons are as angry and bent on annihilation as mine is. I'm observing that the person affects their Dragon as much as it affects them.

The new barista behind the counter has a red Dragon. Her Dragon has feathers and a long, snake-like body with large eyes and a strange beard. It has a kind smile, just like her, and it whispers words of comfort and wisdom to all the patrons. When she first started working I thought she could see the Dragons like I can, but I was wrong. It is only now, in her retirement, that she seems to have let her Dragon out. I can tell by the eagerness with which it greats the customers; she kept it locked in a cage for far too long and its desperation for interaction shows it. I think that's what made mine so angry: keeping it buried and denied for so long. The barista's became desperate to share her knowledge and character, mine became vengeful. I look over to the girl with the blue Dragon and I hope, for her sake, it doesn't take her until her retirement to let her Dragon free from the cage they both have locked themselves in. Otherwise, her sad Dragon might fill with resentment and she will find that neither tea nor bitter coffee can appease it: only something stronger found in dark places can placate it, then.

I don't know what to do, Doctor. I'm not ready to find you yet; I want to figure this out on my own. I am learning about my Dragon more and more, and the relationship between man and Dragon is not what I had thought. I thought one of us had to be in control—one of us had to be dominant, that is the understanding of the world that was beaten into me. Perhaps, like with everything else I'm learning, that too was wrong. Is it possible that together, we can build something new? That doesn't seem right. I don't think my Dragon is capable of building since his first reaction in to destroy—like with that man. The fear I caused in his eyes would have been shameful to you.

Talk to you soon, Doctor.

Me

To: The Doctor with the Glasses

I stopped going to the other coffee shops and public spaces I had been frequenting. It's been a week now since the girl with the silver locket went missing and I can't stop this burning feeling filling me. I thought maybe I'd find the boy with the red hair at another shop. My Dragon led me from place to place, but he was nowhere to be found. My Dragon is growing anxious—I can feel it breathing down my neck with its hot, angry puffs.

It's incredible, Doctor, this secret I have learned. It was the one you were trying to guide me towards, but I couldn't hear it then. I wasn't ready that day in your office when I came face-to-face with my Dragon for the first time. It's so simple, though. I can't believe I didn't see it before.

I can only hope the boy with the red hair doesn't know this secret. If he does, the girl with the silver locket really will be gone forever. Knowing the secret of the Dragon allows you to create anything—build anything. There are no walls or limits here. There are no sticks of reason or logic with which to beat us with. Now I know why you wanted us to reconcile so badly. It is only through the reconciliation of the Dragon and the self that we can enter this space where we are unencumbered by the external and can return to that world we once knew together as a child. This is the world where we can begin to build, to create.

I return to my coffee shop every day. I sit in the same spot, my back against the wall, watching the people as they come in and out of the door. The woman with the blue Dragon has started coming in more frequently, as well. She used to only come on Saturdays, but now she and her sad Dragon come a couple times during the week in the evening, too. She stays for long hours until the sun goes down, her nose pressed in a book or a notepad. I only get a nod when she walks in, to acknowledge the recognition of another regular. She seems weary, Doctor. I wish you were here to help her. Whatever is on her mind, it makes her Dragon build a higher wall around her to keep anyone from ever getting close.

There is nothing I can do for her. The only thing I can do is sit here and wait, letting the creation of a plan build between me and my Dragon.

Talk to you soon, Doctor.

Me

To: The Doctor with the Glasses

I saw him today. The boy with the red hair finally returned to the coffee shop. I've waited for him for weeks now, knowing that one day he would eventually return. Still no sign of the girl with the silver locket, I've been keeping up with the news just for her. They've searched the county high and low, but I know she's not here. His black Dragon flirts with the barista confidently, wrapping the older woman in a similar net of charm and deceit that the young girl had been snatched up by. No, this boy took her far away from here. My Dragon blows smoke out of his nostrils at the sight of the boy with the red hair, but I calm it down. I don't want it to unleash its anger prematurely and ruin the plan we have created. Our reconciliation is still delicate, but without it we will never be able to bring into fruition our creation.

The woman with the blue Dragon looks up at me, her eyes studying me for the first time. We had become familiar with each other's presence, knowing and expecting one another at certain times. She has started to come to the coffee shop even more often now. Her blue Dragon had slowly started to take notice of other people around her, instead of just reading over the girl's shoulder. This was, however, the first time she really looked at me. She'd grown accustomed to me: she'd seen my hair, my eyes, my face. She'd gotten comfortable with me: she'd smile and give a nod in greeting. Now, as my eyes follow the boy with the red hair, I see her face lift and her eyes fix on me in a way they never have before. Out of my peripheral, I notice her finally see my Dragon.

She is shocked, as most people are I imagine. Not only is it a golden Dragon glowing with raw power and energy, but as I said before, Doctor, my kind of Dragon doesn't frequent coffee shops. She is scared, perhaps, and I am sorry for that. I like her enough though we have never spoken, but I can't take the time right now to reassure her; the boy with the red hair is walking away. I stand up, leaving my almost full cup of coffee on the table, and follow him out the door. The girl with the blue Dragon watches me the whole time and I can feel her unspoken questions pelting me like bullets. All I can offer her when I pass by is a sad half-smile, but I am unable to hide the fire in my eyes. Maybe that will answer something.

The boy walks with arrogance. His step is assured and he reeks of so much hubris it takes all the control we have to keep my Dragon at bay just a little longer. The boy doesn't seem to know we're following him—that, or he doesn't care. His Dragon whispers to him that he is untouchable—and he believes it. He half-listens to his Dragon and believes that he is in complete control while his Dragon and I know better.

When he gets in his truck, I let my Dragon out.

"Let's go for a ride." My Dragon says, crawling into the front seat beside him. The boy looks scared, but his Dragon steps in and tries to compensate for it by mouthing off. But my Dragon is older, more experienced, and more practiced than his. My Dragon is angrier, crueler, and more resourceful than his. Most importantly, though, my Dragon knows a secret that his doesn't: he is even more powerful now that we have reconciled and neither of us have to fight for power or control over the other. The black Dragon wants to fight, but the boy with the red hair is too frightened to let it. My Dragon wins.

We go for a ride. It's not a long ride, only an hour or two, but long enough to get out of town. My Dragon is patient and steady, not blowing fire or devouring the boy until it has what it wants. I wait quietly for my time to step in. It is not my turn yet. The boy takes me to a house and parks in front. He keeps his hands on the wheel and his eyes trained forward, but the shaking of his knees tell me that he is scared. His Dragon doesn't know what to do: does it fight? Does it run? Does it go down in flames and take me with it? Luckily for me, the boy allows his fear to repress his Dragon and thus has no solution.

I get out of the truck and follow my Dragon into the house; these are the dark places he's used to finding his absolution. He is familiar with the dim lighting and the unkempt floors. It's a good thing you're not here after all, Doctor. You wouldn't be able to handle the stench, but this is what my Dragon used to call home. The girl with the silver locket isn't hard to find, she's the only one in the house. I found her crumpled body, clothed in dirty garments and her own vomit. Her pink Dragon is frightened but has grown weak after days of trying to get the girl to leave. I recognize the familiar resignation in the pink Dragon's eyes. My Dragon steps aside and lets me take the needle out of her arm gently and scoop her up. She moans a little, and her eyes flutter open partially and then close again. She is too high to maintain consciousness but her Dragon follows us as I carry her out of the house, her head lolling from side to side with each step I take. I'm not prepared for the flashing lights when I step out. I'm not prepared for the onslaught of officers nor the boy with the red hair pressed against a cop car with his hands behind his back.

I had been prepared to steal the truck after my Dragon did with the boy whatever it wanted to do to him. I was going to teach the boy my secret: when you join with your Dragon and take it into you, there is nothing on this planet that can stop you. Nothing you cannot create; nothing you cannot bring into manifestation with words, tools, or will.

Paramedics are taking the girl to the hospital and I'm going in for questioning.

Talk to you soon, Doctor.

Me

To: The Doctor with the Glasses

It was the woman with the blue Dragon. I hadn't expected it to be her; I never could have guessed, but you probably would have. The moment she sat across from me in the interrogation room it all kind of clicked. She is an investigator for the police department and when she saw my Dragon come out and follow the boy with the red hair, she had grown suspicious.

"I watched you leave, and the fire in your eyes told me that you knew something horrible was about to happen. I watched you follow the boy and when you climbed into his truck, I knew something was terribly wrong. I called back-up and had them follow you. When you went into the house, the officer questioned the boy and he confessed everything." She told me. Apparently, the boy with the red hair had coerced

145

the young girl with the silver locket to go with him. She had agreed—at first—to see the fantastical world he promised her. When she told him she wanted to go home, well, the black Dragon wasn't okay with that. I won't give you the details, you don't need them, but he manipulated her to stay. He showed her those toxins so familiar to me which prevented her from listening to her pink Dragon. His black Dragon had kept her drugged so she couldn't leave, but the hospital says that she'll be fine. They'll probably send her to your camp when she's ready to be released. You can help her then, I know you can.

"How did you know it was him?" The woman with the blue Dragon asked me. Her Dragon stood behind her, protecting her from everyone and everything that came through that precinct. I finally understood why she kept the world at arm's length. I would, too, if I had her job.

I wanted to answer her question, but I couldn't. I didn't know how. Nothing about how I was able to find and save the girl with the silver locket was traditional. I didn't use logic the way it had be beaten into us all. Nothing about my methods were conventional, or responsible, or obligated. I listened to my Dragon, I melded with him instead of keeping him separate and let us create a solution together that I never could have seen on my own. I ignored what had been beaten into me, and embraced what had been beaten out of me. I let the magic of imagination, intuition, and ingenuity embrace me and guide me. I combined reason and logic with this magic and let it create something new. How do you explain that to someone who couldn't possibly comprehend this secret? Who hasn't reconciled like we have? So I shrugged in answer because I had no words to say.

The woman with the blue Dragon tilted her head and studied me for the second time. "I can't condone your methods, but you saved that girl's life and I thank you for it.

Her family thanks you for it. You found her just in time to prevent her from getting lost to that world of addiction." She told me.

I stayed silent and stared at her, my eyes flicking over to her Dragon every now and then to ensure that it was still the docile beast I had come to know and recognize. It still had the cold sadness around her, but there was also a steady strength within that self-inflicted isolation that I hadn't seen before. I looked back to the woman with the blue Dragon and smiled. She was going to be fine. One day, her Dragon might tear down all those walls and let that strength carry all the weight of her world instead.

She pursed her lips and leaned back in her chair. "Just answer me this: how did you manage to do what none of the officers here could?" She asked me.

I smiled at her. "I didn't use only logic and strategy." I explained to her. I shared with her the secret of the Dragon: together you have unlimited creation. Once I was done, she stayed silent. She tapped her fingers on the table and I feared she would condemn me as crazy like the judge did five months ago—that's when I first met you, Doctor. My, how time flies. Then, the woman with the blue Dragon's eyes twinkled at me and she stood up to leave. Perhaps maybe, just maybe, she did know the secret, after all.

"I think it's time we got you back to the rehabilitation center you're missing from, Kevin." She told me kindly. She patted my shoulder, her Dragon grinned at me, and then they left. I should have known she'd figured me out.

See you soon, Doctor.

K

147

To: The Doctor with the Glasses

So, Doctor, I am here at the police station, sitting with my Dragon in the front room. I know you've been searching for me, and I'm ready for you to find us now. I have learned how to maintain this reconciliation, and it's not as hard as I thought it was. It's not about controlling the Dragon or letting him control me, it's about creating a partnership. In order to create the impossible, one must embrace the magic within us. It's always been there—that wonderful id that we are conditioned to ignore.

I have reconciled myself completely: my id and ego together. It is not to be without reason and logic—allowing the Dragon to rule and consume only leads to destruction. I know that better than anyone else. Being back in that dark place, holding the girl with the silver locket in my arms, I knew what I had escaped and never want to go back. Contrary to what I thought before, it is not about repressing the Dragon, either. That only leads to emptiness. It is a balance between the two; a balance between logic and magic, reason and fantasy.

I'm waiting for you, Doctor. Once you get here I want to learn all your secrets. I know (now that I've reconciled myself with the Dragon within me and he is destructive no more) that there is so much more we can create. Is it possible to make all the fantasies I dreamt of as child real? I know you have the answers, Doctor. Come find me so we can get started.

See you soon, Doctor.

Kevin.

SEDATED

THOMAS A. FOWLER

Detective Hayley Fumero flicked at the pages of her missing persons file. The setting sun outside left little, natural light in her office. She turned on the desk lamp, preferring a smaller, warm light to the cold, overhead fluorescents installed in the building. She scanned the last social media post Lindsay Brice shared before her disappearance: Saturday night, local bar. The picture posted less than an hour before last call. Her missing person was under 21. Fumero wondered how intentional the bar's age check was. Bar owners knew young women in their bar attracted business and known to look the other way when checking at the door. But Fumero's instinct said there was more than putting desirable customers in their bar. She gathered five files, turned off her desk lamp, and headed for her captain's office. She caught him packing his bag, just before leaving for the day.

Fumero knocked on his door.

"Come in."

"Are you sure? Don't want to disturb you if you're headed out."

"No trouble. What have you got for me?" he asked.

"We've seen six females disappear in the last three weeks. Five of them have patterns that are way too similar. All age 18 to 20. Highest education level at high school, enrolled in an Associate's program at best." Fumero handed him the five files for her case. "All disappeared from bars or nightclubs, or shortly after visiting one. All within a twenty-mile radius."

"Do you think we have a serial kidnapper on our hands? Or..." Captain Morris paused. "You aren't bringing the Walsh case back up, are you?"

"Sir, I know you told me to dismiss it. I know that we've engaged the Feds to no avail, but I firmly believe there's a human trafficking network being setup in our town. The common patterns are too familiar." Fumero handed him another file, profiling disappearances in another city. Then another file showing recent cases in their own. "No one thinks it happens in their hometown, but it does. With the gentrification we're seeing an increase in young people moving in, but it's not so busy we can afford a special unit. It's prime for the area. I'd like to look for physical evidence before the trail goes cold."

Captain Morris looked over the two city profiles. His fingers tapped the maps, comparing over the vans used for transporting. "Pursue it. But nothing about human trafficking or the Walsh case is entered officially until you find me something tangible."

"Absolutely," Fumero gathered her files, putting them all together. Each one coded for its unique contribution to the case.

"If you are that set on it, it's at least worth giving you a shot. I've learned by now to trust when you have a hunch."

The captain grabbed his keys and checked his cell phone, taking a moment to think before giving his final instructions. "Bring Koven, he's your secondary. For all he's concerned, nothing related to human trafficking, don't need the Feds hearing we're back on it. Treat it as a potential serial case. The profile matches and could be your end result, anyway, if it isn't trafficking. But that angle will keep you looking for the right clues."

"Absolutely. Thank you, Captain," Fumero said.

While Fumero drove to the bar, Koven sat beside her. He thumbed over the photographs of Lindsay Brice. "2,300 people are reported missing every day, Fumero. You think these five are connected?"

"You don't?" Fumero asked.

"You're on to something. The dots are there. Key is finding what connects them." Koven pointed at the Brice post. "Did we interview this bartender?"

"Brandt Hotham. Everyone calls him 'Bunny.' Claims the doorman checked ID, threw the blame his way so he 'didn't know' he was serving underage," Fumero said.

"You believe him?" Koven asked.

"Worth a second conversation."

They parked a fair distance from the bar. The sun set behind the buildings against a darkening blue sky. The neon sign flickered above the bar, Valve. Fumero scanned the area, noticing a connecting hallway from Valve to another building. She turned off the engine, she and Koven settled in to scan the area.

"Do we know what that connected facility is?" Fumero asked, pointing at the connecting hallway through the windshield. She'd want to find that door once they were inside.

"This place distills its own gin, it's why it's so well known around town," Koven shook his head, incredulous that she even had to ask. "Haven't you been here?"

"No, you know I haven't. I don't go anywhere that loud and insane," she replied.

"You're what? Two years older than me?" Koven opened the compartment between the front seats. "How do you not have anything stocked to eat? Do you even go on stakeouts?"

"In years, yes. But it doesn't reflect your man-child soul. Mine is much wiser and not up for the kids and their loud music." Fumero pulled a protein bar from her purse. "And yes, I go on stakeouts, but I don't keep a trough to sort through."

"So if you don't go to clubs, what do you do? Puzzles and watch 'Golden Girls?'" Koven moved through his smart phone, pulling up reports on the building to check for suspicious activity or previous arrests in the area.

"Like hell I'm going to tell you," Fumero took a bite from her own bar. "Plus, what's wrong with 'The Golden Girls?' That show is amazing!"

"Ha! Knew it!" Koven smiled, taking another bite of his protein bar. He kept his attention on his search results.

"I don't do puzzles. My life and spirit just demand simplicity—and my closest friends, thank you," Fumero said. "That's all you get to know."

"Hey, it can go both ways. What do you want to know about me?" Koven asked.

"How's the new place?" she took one massive bite, taking down the rest of her protein bar.

"Oh, not bad. Going to be more work to fix up than I thought, but it'll be worth it once it's done, property value increases, nice view." Koven continued, "But I'm looking forward to having a nice place I can get up and run, not a shithole by the river."

"There's the dream. To not have a shithole by the river. What's the scoop?" Fumero asked.

"I was right. Building is a warehouse zoned and permitted for alcohol distribution. Established three years before Valve. Only recorded incident at the facility concerns an altercation between two employees. No formal charges filed. Bar has had some usual drunken fights local patrol broke up, few temporary lockups. No formal assault charges or anything. Two reported sexual harassment claims."

"Anything on the staff?" Fumero asked.

"Looking." Koven scrolled. "Last filing eight months ago."

Fumero analyzed the long hallway between the bar itself and the distribution plant. No windows, no access doors. A long hallway with nothing to it.

"Patron acting too aggressive," Koven continued moving through the results. "Similar report, arrest for drunk and disorderly after multiple females reported aggressive behavior and unwanted physical contact. Was thrown out by bouncer, when aggressive suspect tried to work his way back in, bouncer fought back, that's when cops were called. So still civilian-related, even when staff are on reports they seem to follow standard protocol."

"I'll talk to Hotham," Fumero said.

"Bunny?" Koven teased.

"Yes, Bunny," Fumero replied. "You look around. See how the distribution plant is connected."

"You interviewed him the first time, sure you don't want to mix it up?" Koven asked.

She put on a false, flirty smile, playing the part to lure information. "Bartenders are always willing to talk to a pretty face like me," Fumero opened the car door.

"Can't argue with that. Men are both horny and stupid. I should know, being a horny and stupid male myself." Koven ate the last bite of his protein bar, then followed her out of the car. "Although, because I know you, that look is creepy, doesn't suit you."

"But the big strong man doesn't know that." Fumero teased. They strode toward the building; Fumero stopped smiling as they approached the bar and she stopped "playing her character."

"You check out the distillery, find out how it connects to the bar and see if there is anyone you can question while I chat with our bartender again." Fumero pointed toward the neighboring building, directing Koven.

Koven nodded, heading toward the long corridor and the distillery while Fumero stepped inside the bar.

A few people had drinks; standard crowd for early on a weeknight. Most looked like regulars in their middle age, not wanting to go home yet. Fumero saw Hotham step into the back.

"Mr. Hotham?" Fumero called after him.

He whispered to a fellow bartender, a towering man with black hair, before turning back around toward Fumero.

"What can I do for you, Detective...?" Hotham paused.

"Fumero."

"Fumero, yes, that was it," Hotham said. "Care for a drink?"

"No thank you," Fumero replied. "Wanted to ask you a bit more about Lindsay Brice."

"Sure," Hotham asked.

Without shifting her focus from 'Bunny,' Fumero caught, out of the corner of her eye, the black-haired bartender head west toward the distribution center.

"There's a pattern of missing persons in bars around town," Fumero said. "Wanted to see if you knew anything about these other disappearances."

"Sure," Hotham said.

"Have you seen any suspicious individuals, or had to remove anyone for sexually aggressive behavior, antagonizing female attendees, anything of that sort?" Fumero asked.

"Apart from the usual creepo we have to kick out, can't think of anything," Hotham replied. "I assume you're looking for unusual behavior."

"Well, any unwanted advances should be considered unusual, but yes, I'm talking about individuals seeming off-kilter, perhaps asking about women in the bar, anyone trying to cull information or perhaps learn lifestyle patterns, behaviors, or habits," Fumero said.

"There was a guy, he asked about a girl and whether she was single," Hotham said. "Then he started asking where she worked and what she liked."

"Did you know who the girl was he was interested in?" Fumero asked.

"No, wasn't a regular or anything. Seemed like the guy was looking for an icebreaker or conversation starter or something," he said. Hotham looked back toward the distribution center hall. The towering man with black hair had returned. Hotham shook his head, signaling the man back. "Not right now," Hotham said.

"What's not right now?" Fumero asked.

"Oh," Hotham cleared his throat. "We need another keg for the tap, tonight's Ladies Night. Figured he should wait until we're done."

"No, don't worry, you can take care of that while we chat," Fumero noticed the odd pause. The throat clear didn't seem necessary, almost like it was to delay his response. Fumero wondered why Hotham delayed his answer. He could've been making it up, and if that were the case, Fumero wasn't sure what the towering man was supposed to have been doing instead and she was very interested in finding out.

"Go ahead, grab the keg so we can swap it out. Full kegs are on the left side of the warehouse," Hotham directed.

"Has he worked here long?" Fumero asked, watching the tall man do as Hotham directed.

"Been here a few months," Hotham replied.

"And he doesn't know where to find a keg?" Fumero asked, watching his eyes look down at the bar, avoiding answering the question.

Hotham cleared his throat again. He grabbed a glass, sipping from it. "One second."

"No, please," Fumero let him take a moment, showing how nervous he was getting as he stared into the water he drank from.

"Something in my throat." He put his glass down and wiped his mouth. "You sure you don't want a drink? I'm trying a new gin cocktail for Ladies Night."

"No, thank you," Fumero said.

"Gin not the right kind of drink for a lady like you?" Hotham asked.

"No, not the right company," Fumero smiled at the bartender, letting him know she didn't prefer his company one bit.

"Okay, okay," Hotham raised his hands in the air. "Just trying to be nice. To answer your question: we just rearranged the warehouse a bit, so he hasn't been able to really get oriented since we cleaned up last week."

What she intended for routine questions turned into a lead. "After this man asked about the girl, whether she was single, had any interests, I assume you couldn't tell him anything…"

"No, didn't know who she was so I told him sorry, he was on his own."

"After your conversation, did you see if he tried hitting on her?"

"Yeah, he gave it a shot anyway," Hotham said, flippantly.

"How long did they talk and did they leave together?"

"Don't think the conversation was long, she seemed pretty uninterested." Hotham refilled his glass but didn't take another sip. "It was pretty busy so I didn't pay attention to much going on. Just the occasional sweep to make sure everyone was behaving."

"Can you give me a name and description of the man you described?" Fumero brought out her notepad, ready to jot it down.

"Name, not really."

"Didn't you check his ID?"

"You expect me to remember names once I see they're old enough to drink? I see dozens of those an hour," Hotham gave a dry chuckle. "Could maybe look at tabs and receipts, but couldn't pick the name out, necessarily."

"Okay, what about his age, size, build, all of that?"

"Eh, normal guy. White. He was probably in his late-thirties, early-forties, scruff, not a beard," Hotham described.

The towering man returned with a keg on a dolly. He pushed it up to the bar.

"Bring it closer, I don't want to carry it that far," Hotham instructed, waving the guy forward.

The towering man looked at the dolly and back to the bar, confused by the raise of the padded floor behind the bar to absorb liquid.

"Here, let me help," Hotham helped the towering man with the dolly.

The guy seemed unfamiliar with regular processes, which was odd for an employee having been there for a few months.

"Um, the guy had light brown hair, little overweight, I'd say 200-220 pounds," Hotham continued as he lifted the dolly over the lip of the pad.

The empty keg hissed as they unhooked it. The "empty" keg seemed almost as heavy as its replacement. Hotham and the towering man with black hair heaved it down to the floor, then put the new one in with almost the same effort. Keg shells weren't inherently heavy. They gained their weight from volume.

"Bad keg?" Fumero asked.

"Huh?" Hotham replied.

"Well, keg you're replacing seems pretty full, must've gone bad," Fumero pointed out.

"Oh, yeah, coming out flatter than a pancake," Hotham said.

"Pressure released when you unhooked it from the tap," Fumero said. "The hissing sounded like it had plenty of CO_2."

"Ya know, maybe a faulty valve or something," Hotham said.

Fumero's cell phone buzzed. She pulled it from her pocket. A text arrived from Captain Morris.

Urgent. Just received from Cyber Crimes. Different bar. The Barreling Cask. Three nights before Brice disappearance.

A text from Koven.

Headed to you from distillery. Backup en route.

Her service bar was low, something interfered with the signal. She didn't have that problem outside the bar, her and Koven were able to load the case files and research no problem. The picture the captain texted her loaded slowly. It was pixelated, buffering as it processed the data. She ignored it, allowing it to load while she continued the conversation.

"If the valve is faulty then how did the CO2 have pressure?" Fumero asked.

"Sometimes a keg goes bad," Hotham said. Sweat dripped from his brow, an excessive amount for a few moments of lifting. Face flushed red.

"Okay," Fumero said.

She waited for the picture to load. Another text came from the captain.

Social post from Cynthia Vargas. Night of her disappearance. Removed from user history.

The picture finished loading. In the image, Cynthia danced with friends at the bar she disappeared from. Behind the counter, a familiar face poured drinks. She glanced one more time to be sure it was Hotham. No denying it with the long, strawberry blonde hair. And sitting at the bar, not far away from Cynthia, was a towering man with black hair.

A final text from Koven.

Twenty seconds. Backup nearly here, too.

"When the man who asked about, then hit on the girl, did you see him leave?" Fumero moved her hand near her pistol, careful not to draw attention by resting her hand on her thigh, avoiding any obvious reach for her weapon.

"He paid his bill, not sure if he stuck around or took off right away," Hotham finished with the keg. His eyes looked down, somewhere below the bar. Scanning for something, Fumero had a solid idea what he was making sure was where he remembered it.

"Fair enough, anything else you can think of about this man, or any other suspicious individuals you can think of?" Fumero moved her hand as close to her pistol as possible without looking obvious.

"Not a thing." He wiped his forehead with a white rag. "We only see the usual bar nuts every now and then." Hotham coughed again. "Sure you don't want a drink?"

"You know, it's already been a hell of a week." Fumero scanned the bottles on the shelves behind Hotham, looking for something to keep his hands high and visible while she kept him occupied. "How about a Seven and Seven?"

"Sure," he said, brow wrinkled in confusion by the change motion.

The bar door opened. Koven entered, acting casual as ever. He scratched his forehead with only his pointer finger. Then as he brought his hand down, he made the ASL sign for 'M.'

1M. One minute until backup arrived. Fumero watched both the towering man and Hotham carefully. Hotham reached for the bottle of Seagram's Seven Crown Whiskey. Hotham worked on the drink as he greeted Koven. "Be with you in a minute."

"Absolutely, ladies first," Koven nodded at Fumero. They exchanged a smile, acting as if they didn't know one another. Smartly, he sat at the other end of the bar, creating some space between him and Fumero, giving them two vantage points to cover the bar. He sat on his barstool but turned to lean his back against the bar itself. It let him look outside to watch for backup.

After Hotham served Fumero, he walked down to the other end. Koven saw backup arriving.

"You ready for a drink?" Hotham asked.

"Yep," Koven said, spinning around on the barstool. Right as he turned, he looked at Fumero. "Ready to get things going."

Hotham was far from the gun he looked under the bar for earlier. Timing was perfect.

"Tell me, Mr. Hotham." Fumero gripped her pistol sheathed in the holster strapped to her hip. "Do you have multiple jobs?"

"Yep, believe it or not, bartending doesn't pay the bills too well," Hotham said.

"Do you work over at The Barreling Cask?" Fumero turned off the safety. "Is that why they call you 'Bunny?'"

The towering man stopped getting the "faulty" keg onto the dolly. He looked up at Fumero.

"Because I hop from bar to bar," Hotham said.

Fumero nodded to Koven. The two drew their weapons. Koven at the nearby Hotham. Fumero at the towering man.

"DPD, hands where I can see them!" Fumero shouted.

The towering man did so without hesitation. Hotham moved slower, defiantly smiling at Fumero, then turning his attention to Koven. "You too?"

"DPD, you heard the woman," Koven kept his barrel pointed right at Hotham.

Cops entered the front door. "DPD!"

"Officers, get these civilians out." Fumero continued, "Verify IDs and run backgrounds before releasing them."

"You heard the detective, everyone out," an officer commanded.

The officers escorted the regulars out. One patron hesitated, but it was because he was scared out of his mind. Fumero figured the guy had priors or was on parole feared he'd be guilty by association, maybe had a bench warrant. Regardless, it wasn't the face of an innocent man.

"Be right back," the officer replied. "Give us a second to get these gentlemen and women comfortable."

Fumero nodded. "Thank you, officer." She shifted the conversation to the towering man. "Is the door to that back hallway locked?"

The towering man nodded.

"Do you have the keys?" Fumero, gun still trained on him, nudged her head toward the door.

"I can't," he replied.

"It's getting opened one way or another," Fumero said. "Do you want to cooperate, or would you like to add obstruction to your charges?"

"You don't have shit on us," Hotham said.

"I've got pictures of you standing behind Cynthia Vargas the night of her disappearance. I've got Lindsey Brice's last known location to be here," Fumero said. "Keep your hands where I can see them, step out from behind the bar."

The hallway door opened. Koven and Fumero looked over, keeping their guns on their respective suspects. Men dressed in black emerged from the hall, instantly firing on them. Koven ducked behind the curved corner of the bar. Fumero had few options. She jumped toward a massive metal support beam, covered behind it. A bullet grazed her leather jacket, ripping the fabric and seam on the shoulder. The impact spun her around, even from the mild graze. Falling behind the beam, she ducked down. She looked over at the bar just in time to see Hotham reaching under it. His's arms swung up, shotgun in hand.

162

Fumero fired two rounds, shooting through the bar counter. Wood and glass shattered. The bullets thrust Hotham back. He crashed into the bottles behind him, tumbling to the ground with broken glass and dripping alcohol. The towering man bolted for the warehouse, using the two men dressed in black's covering fire to make his escape. As the officers came pouring in from the outside, the towering man and men in black retreated into the hallway. The room went silent, except for Hotham's groans of agony.

Fumero hopped over the bar, pistol still raised. "Officers, make sure the west exits of the distillery are covered. Those three don't leave! Koven and I will take this entrance."

Their backup left. Hotham clutched at his bullet wounds, bleeding but not dead. Fumero kicked the shotgun away.

"Contact. Shots fired," Fumero radioed. "Three suspects entered hallway headed west toward distillery. Primary suspect is six foot three, two hundred and fifty pounds. Caucasian, black hair. Keep all bargoers for questioning, need to make sure they weren't plants."

She secured handcuffs on Hotham, then searched him. They pulled his wallet, cell phone, a second burner cell phone, and a set of keys.

"Which one unlocks the door?" Fumero asked.

Hotham turned his head, staring at the outside as he ran his tongue defiantly against his teeth.

"It's going to be like that?" Fumero asked.

Hotham didn't answer. Fumero stood, Koven followed her. He took the keys to start working through the baker's dozen worth of possibilities.

"Dispatch, need ambulance on my location," Fumero radioed. "Two gunshot wounds. Suspect is conscious but bleeding, cannot stay. In pursuit of another suspect."

"You hit?" Koven asked, trying the second key.

"Grazed the jacket, I'm okay," Fumero said.

The third key failed. The fourth worked.

Koven and Fumero opened the hallway door to advance on the distribution center, she saw the black-haired suspect hunkered down behind a bunch of crates. Koven provided covering fire. Fumero fell against the right side of the hallway. She took cover behind some kegs. Koven pushed back against the left side of the door frame. The tall man blindly shot up at the ceiling. Little precision or calculation to his actions, he was more panicked than she normally saw for a henchman within organized crime. After emptying his clip, Fumero advanced while he clumsily reloaded. Moving toward him, he shook to the point he dropped his replacement clip. She stepped around the crates, gun right on him. She announced her position to the suspect.

"DPD Detective. Freeze."

The suspect kept his pistol in hand, but his tensed in his crouched posture, letting her know he had heard her.

"One move with that pistol toward me, or my partner, and you're dead before your body hits the ground," Fumero said.

The towering man with black hair dropped the gun, and raised his hands.

"Please," he begged while she yanked his hands down, pulling them tightly behind his back as she handcuffed him.

Koven secured the area. The windows to the outside lit up with blue and red flashing lights as squad cars surrounded the area.

"Show us where they are," Fumero said. "We're going to sweep the area. Might as well get us to the missing girls. It'll look a hell of a lot better on my report if you cooperate."

"Doesn't matter. I'm dead anyway. Stairwell, southeast corner."

"Am I going to find anything I shouldn't?" Fumero asked, frisking him for additional weapons.

"Wallet, keys and phone," the towering man said. "And chapstick."

Sure enough, she found a stick of tea tree and raspberry chapstick. She felt something even thinner in his jacket pockets. She pulled out three, clear tubes. They'd been cut and appeared to be remnants.

"What are these for?" Fumero asked.

"Tubing for a water pump," he replied.

"Awfully thin to move water through. What do you mean you're dead anyway?" Fumero asked.

"They won't risk me telling you more than you're about to find," the towering man said. "Comes with the deal."

Fumero looked at the towering man, sweating, breathing heavy, overcome with a sense of dread mixed with acceptance.

"You'd better get down there. They may try to move the girls out or kill them to avoid having more witnesses," he said.

Fumero bolted for the stairwell.

Koven met up with her, they entered the warehouse basement. Multiple liquor storage units lined the walls. Koven had his pistol aimed to the right, Fumero covered the left with hers.

"He led us to nowhere," Koven said.

Fumero shook her head. "Quiet."

Panicked voices. Muffled. She couldn't make out where they came from. Then one particularly stressed voice gave the position away. Fumero pointed at the far-west wall, it was more liquor, stored against tall, wooden shelving.

Koven and Fumero advanced.

"Watch our six," Fumero said.

Koven turned. They pushed their shoulders together, moving as one toward the west wall. The voices became easier to hear, she couldn't hear the articulation of anything, but something was on the other side. Koven kept his pistol pointed toward the stairwell, in case anyone chased after them from the way they came. Fumero took one more step, grasping the wooden framing of the liquor storage. She put her hand on Koven's back, letting him know to stop.

"No sign of movement on my end," Koven said.

"I push, you clear right," Fumero said. "Right behind you on the left side."

"Right side. Your move," Koven said. He turned, pistol pointed toward the storage unit.

Fumero pushed the storage with all her strength. It swung open. She ducked and pushed the door as far as possible to give Koven a clear entry.

"DPD. Nobody move!" Koven shouted.

The massive, hidden door slammed into the left wall. Fumero swung around.

Koven fired his weapon. There was return fire. A bullet grazed his shoulder. Red sprayed against the back wall.

Fumero knelt, aiming up at the direction of fire. She saw an enforcer duck behind a stretcher. Lindsay Brice was on the stretcher, strapped down, unconscious.

Koven knelt behind a crate of liquor, tearing his sleeve to inspect and deal with the gunshot wound.

Fumero aimed under the stretcher. Crosshairs pointed between the hydraulic jacks and the descent valve. The metal supports of the medical stretcher gave her a small window. She fired once. The pistol recoiled. Seven shots left.

The gunman groaned, agonizing from the wound. Still, he swung his pistol up, firing at Fumero's direction.

Fumero ducked behind the door. Bottles shattered. Liquor flew everywhere.

"I've got 'em pinned. Go!" The gunman shouted.

Koven swung back up, firing at two more enforcers trying to take more stretchers toward a nearby loading dock.

Fumero thought of doing a few, blind, cover shots to give Koven a few moments to aim his shots, but couldn't risk hitting any of the women tethered to the stretchers. Her mind was made up: it wasn't worth the risk. She fired up at the ceiling to give covering fire.

"Advancing," Koven shouted.

Fumero ducked, coming out from behind the door. Pistol aimed at the gunman.

He limped back toward the warehouse loading dock, trying to drag Hoto and the stretcher with him. He fired, but without precision.

Fumero took one more shot, hitting the gunman in his shoulder. The gunman dropped the pistol and fell to the ground.

Koven shouted at the other two enforcers. "Let go of the stretchers or I will fire." Fumero bolted toward the gunman, kicking the pistol toward the back wall and away from the suspect. She kept her gun trained on the fleeing enforcers. One let his stretcher go. The other tried to make a break for it with what looked like Veronica Aguilar.

Koven made good on his promise. He fired one round. It clipped the enforcer in the shoulder. After dropping to the floor, he stood back up with help from his fellow enforcer, the two ran for the exit.

The faint light from the streetlamps outside warehouse loading dock changed to flashing blue and red. As the enforcers disappeared from Fumero and Koven's view, they could hear other officers, outside the loading dock, shout commands to freeze.

Fumero and Koven kept their pistols on the exit in case the enforcers tried to double back. Koven's breathing became heavy, his nerves shot, and adrenaline on high alert. Fumero's pistol shivered. The let down of adrenaline was starting. For the attack, she kept calm, did what she had to. Now that the victims were safe and last of the enforcers apprehended, her body knew it was time to crash.

"Status on suspects?" Fumero asked.

"Two in custody," an officer shouted.

More officers came in, weapons drawn.

"Sweep the area. Looking for suspects only, then we get forensics down here and bag evidence," Fumero said. She turned to her radio. "Dispatch, additional ambulances needed at location of shoot-out. Two additional suspects with gunshot wounds and multiple abduction victims needing assistance."

"I see Hoto and Aguilar." Koven stood over the two stretchers the enforcers tried to take with them.

Fumero approach the other cluster of four stretchers. Six altogether. Each setup had an IV drip trickling into their veins, full heart monitors displayed standard vitals, although they were lower than normal. They were sedated— likely because it was right before transportation to a new location.

She looked at the first victim, asleep and restrained. "Cynthia Vargas."

Fumero moved to another stretcher. A redhead with snow-pale skin. "Gretchen Tate."

The third stretcher was an unfamiliar face. Another missing person, but someone who hadn't been reported. "Unidentified female. Not on our roster of abducted individuals."

The final stretcher among the cluster. Fumero sighed as she began to cry. "Linds..."

The adrenaline in her system sent a warm surge through her body. Her torso flushed as her legs shook. "Lindsa..."

"Lindsay Brice," Koven said. He came over, clenching her shoulders with his hands. "Hey, come on. Let's sit down. We both need to."

They did.

"It's all good. None of the girls were taken out of here," Koven said.

Fumero nodded. "Good shooting. Now we have, what? Five suspects?"

Koven counted. "Two guys down by the loader. Gunman there on the floor you stopped. Beanpole up there and Bunny in the bar. Yeah, five suspects, all alive."

"Can't imagine they're all paid enou..." Fumero stopped to breathe. "All paid enough to keep quiet."

"No, at least one of them will turn for us," Koven said. "Take it easy. Okay? Here, let's both get our firearms put away. We're both shaking."

Fumero had to use both hands to guide the pistol into her holster. Medics arrived, taking vitals and checking all five victims.

"If they're being used for trafficking, why are they sedated?" Koven asked.

"Staging facility, keep them under and hidden until they can be moved," Fumero said. "Heart monitors make sure they're kept under without risking heart failure. Easily awakened and arrive ready for delivery."

Fumero stood up. She walked over to Lindsay Brice. Taking her hand, she remained still, holding her hand until the medics could take them to the loading bay and get them to a hospital.

"Do you think they'll regain consciousness before being taken to Central?" Fumero asked.

"We called in to the hospital. Anesthesia has to assess first, make sure there's no harm in stopping the drip so they come out coherent. After an initial scan, we don't know what the exact cocktail is to keep them sedated," the medic replied. "Don't want to take any chances."

They wheeled Lindsay away. Before they took the others, Fumero walked around to each stretcher, putting their hand in hers, giving them a sense of control and comfort the only way she knew how for the time being.

Koven was taken to the same hospital for treatment of his gunshot. After a while, Fumero hardly recognized anyone. A few people from forensics, one cop who showed up at a previous scene. That was it. She sat alone, the area closed off, civilians looking at the bar and distribution center from behind the barrier, taking photos and videos with their cellphones. News crews gathered to cover what they could. Officers gave them vague answers as they ushered them from the area. She waited for Koven as long as she could, but all the activity made her anxious. She wanted answers.

Her phone chimed. It was the captain.

Return to precinct, need to file report.

Fumero released a sigh and headed back, leaving Koven to get patched up on his own. As she walked up the steps to the precinct, a duo of black, matching SUVs pulled up to the area. Several FBI agents stepped out.

"Fumero," the captain said, meeting the three of them at the door.

She climbed up the final steps toward him, exhausted and starving. At this point she wanted nothing more than a bath, then mindless sitcoms, and a cheeseburger with an abundance of bacon and cheese.

"Fumero, these are agents..." the captain said. He gestured toward the two federal agents. One a middle-aged man with salt and pepper hair, a thin beard to match. The other, a woman in her mid-thirties, pale skin, hair and eyes both dark brown.

"Michaels and Dhavernas, I remember," Fumero said. "You two took the Walsh case from me."

"Yes, they're here to get what they can, information-wise," the captain said. He led the three of them upstairs to the conference room. He held his hand out and motioned for them all to take a seat, closing the door behind them.

"We're also here to inform you the Walsh case has been reopened," Dhavernas said shifting in her chair. Her calm, quiet voice nearly indiscernible with the ringing that persisted in Fumero's ears, echoing from the noise of the scene. "Well..."

"To be fair, it was never really closed," Michaels clarified. "We closed it from your jurisdiction as we looked into a trafficking organization tied to the Walsh case. This distribution center is directly connected, one of the smaller silos feeding a larger base of operations we're trying to hunt down." Dhavernas leaned forward, a stern yet impressed frown on his face. "You brought the Walsh case to us when we didn't even see it was connected. You put the pieces together with Aguilar, Brice, Hoto, Reitzell, Tate, and Vargas."

"Reitzell, was that the sixth abductee?" Fumero asked.

"It was. Identified at the hospital. You weren't investigating Reitzell?" Dhavernas asked.

"No, we had a sixth missing person's case, but it wasn't her. Nothing had been filed or reported with Reitzell," Fumero said. "Found her when we found the others."

"You're saving people and putting the pieces together faster than we've been able to," Michaels said.

"We need you on this case, starting with finding who's been sedating these girls," Dhavernas said.

"Not many people with specialties like that," Fumero said. "It'd have to be a doctor, specialty training, likely in a financial need or background of misconduct would be where we start."

"Exactly, the suspects apprehended tonight are all enforcers, or spotters helping to locate and abduct victims," Dhavernas said. "If we can find this doctor, we'll finally be able to stop raiding individual silos and have our first, major player to locate the base of organization where all of this is happening."

"So what do you think? Care to help out us clueless FBI for a bit? Get the Walsh case solved properly?" Michaels asked.

"Wait!" Fumero put her hands up, asking for everyone to be quiet. "The tubing."

"Tubing?" the Captain asked.

"One of the suspects, I pulled it from his jacket. It was thin, I didn't put it together because we hadn't found the girls. But it was the same tubing used in the IV drips," Fumero said. "It was the tall guy. He told me he was already dead."

"You thinking he's our doctor?" Dhavernas asked.

"Yes, the sixth missing person," Fumero said. "There was a sixth missing person that didn't match the rest of the women taken."

"You found her with the other five, didn't you?" the Captain said.

"No, we had another case with a description very far removed from matching traits of the girls found tonight. Reitzell could've been sold off by her family or didn't have any family so it went unnoticed. The sixth missing reports case I wasn't working. It was someone in their forties, well-to-do lifestyle," Fumero said. She pulled out her phone, calling a fellow detective. She asked for a profile. After several minutes of exchange, she hung up.

"The sixth woman was Ellie Sanderson, the ex-wife of a Doctor George Muth." Fumero pulled up Doctor Muth's practice on the web. In a picture with patients, stood a towering man with black hair. "He had a drop on Koven, a clean shot, but when he fired he acted like he didn't know what he was doing. He put the gun down without a fight, everyone else fled or shot back. We need to find his ex-wife and put Doctor Muth in isolated protection immediately. Where is he?"

"I don't know. Sergeant!" the captain opened the door and shouted at the nearest officer.

The sergeant on duty jogged over to the group. "Yes, Captain?"

"What's the status on all of our suspects from the distillery?" the captain asked.

"The suspects who were shot left in separate ambulances. Two uninjured suspects were put in a squad car," the sergeant reported.

"Call the detention center. One of the suspects without ID is a tall man," Captain Morris, turning to Fumero to fill in the details.

"Suspect is six feet, three inches, thin build, black hair. He has to be put in isolation and questioned immediately," Fumero said.

Dhavernas and Michaels led Fumero and the captain out of the precinct and toward the FBI SUVs. The captain explained the situation to the sergeant as they walked.

"We believe we have another missing case tied to this one that we need to solve now. Once this incident becomes public, it's likely that missing person is going to be killed. Our suspect was working to keep that person safe," the captain said. "We're headed down there now to talk to the suspect. Meantime, have your men do another sweep of the facility, check every corner for potential storage, hidden closets, we'll relay you details of the missing person on the way."

The captain shut the door of the SUV once they had climbed in. The sergeant barked orders, directing other agents to follow the captain's instruction. Junior agents piled in and took the second vehicle.

Dhavernas turned on the siren and flashing lights. The Captain relayed info to dispatch.

"There is a suspect either in lockup or being processed. It is vital the man fitting this description is isolated immediately," the captain said.

As he described the doctor, Fumero became angry. Angry at herself for not putting the pieces together sooner. She shut her eyes as the red and blue lights on the SUV spun above, shining into the window against a pitch-black sky.

"Hey," Dhavernas said. The female agent looked back at Fumero. "I know that look. You were in a high-pressure situation. You can't be expected to put every piece in place while you're taking gunfire. We're going to do everything we can, as quickly as we can."

"Plus, you were the one to put that together. Evidence confiscated the tubing, forensics classified it. Plenty of other people saw those tubes and didn't put it together," Michaels added.

Fumero nodded. "Thank you."

"This is Captain Morris, any word on our suspect, over?" he radioed.

"Negative," the dispatcher replied. "Busy night, over."

"I'll try the sergeant, talk to the squad car that was taking him," the captain said.

Dhavernas honked her horn, despite the siren blaring. Seatbelts tightened across their shoulders as she braked hard.

"This is Three-William-56, over," someone radioed.

"Yes, this is Detective Fumero. You had two suspects headed to lockup from the shootout at the bar on Jefferson, correct? Over." she asked.

"Rodger that, just left. Over," the officer said.

"Was the tall man put into isolation? He remains a suspect but could be a potential key witness next to an enforcer. Over." Fumero asked.

"Not sure. Want me to head back in, make sure? Sounds a little urgent. Over," the officer asked.

"Yes, over," Fumero said. "Officer?"

"Weathers, over," he replied. "I've got you, will make sure he's safe."

"Captain Morris, this is Dispatch, receiving reports of prisoner-induced riot breaking out. You're headed into some chop," they said.

"Copy that, Dispatch," the captain said.

Dhavernas reached another light. Red. She slowed enough to scan the intersection, make sure everyone heard the sirens or saw the lights and yielded.

"How much further?" Dhavneras asked.

"Two blocks up, turn right. It'll be the second building on the left," the captain said.

As they pulled up, they could see Weathers' car near the side entrance. Dhavernas, Michaels, Captain Morris, and Fumero stormed inside.

Several officers inside the detention center fought to keep prisoners back. The inmates, going through processing, pushed against one another. Shouting, cursing, throwing fists, crumbling to the ground. Beyond the main chaos, Weathers had Muth, moving toward the end of the hall. One man, the enforcer from the distribution warehouse, charged after him among the chaos.

"FBI, everybody down," Dhavernas' quiet voice suddenly had a boom. "Warning shots!" She shouted to let the other officers know what was coming.

Dhavernas pulled the trigger on her pistol. Once the shots fired, all prisoners tumbled to the ground, shoving each other to get their faces on the floor and hands behind their head. All but one. The enforcer charged after Weathers and Muth.

"Weathers, heads up!" Fumero pulled her pistol. She aimed carefully, making sure no one else would be harmed tonight. As the enforcer charged Weathers with a shiv, Fumero fired twice. Both in the upper torso. One hit the lungs, the other the heart. The enforcer was dead before his body crumpled to the floor.

"Clear!" Fumero shouted.

"Clear!" a detention officer shouted.

"Weathers?" Fumero asked, running toward him and Muth.

"I'm good, thank you," Weathers said. "I thought it sounded a little urgent."

"Sorry, it was a big urgent," Fumero said.

"Next time give me a heads up," Weathers replied.

"Will do." Fumero turned her attention. "Doctor Muth, right?"

He didn't answer.

"Your ex-wife went missing several weeks ago. If they're holding her captive somewhere, once they get word you've been arrested and the warehouse raided, they're going to kill her. Now's the time to talk."

His lips quivered, drops of sweat fell from his receding hairline.

"I don't know where they're holding her," Muth said.

Dhavernas and the captain made their way over the prisoners on the floor, being guided one at a time by the detention officers to resume processing.

"Did they give any hints? Did you hear her on the phone telling you she'd been taken captive? Did they send a ransom of any kind? Kidnap you together? Anything you can tell us," Fumero asked, helping him stand.

"They sent a picture," Muth said. "It was dark, but I saw shelving like the one in the bar. There wasn't much, but there were bottles."

"Cynthia Vargas. She was in a bar where Hotham and Muth were in the picture," Fumero said. She pulled up her cell phone to look over the texts from Koven. "The Barreling Cask."

"On it," the captain said. "Dispatch, I need any patrol car in the vicinity of The Barreling Cask, a bar."

The captain and Michaels stepped out of the building to work with dispatch, getting away from the noise of the prisoners and detention officers. They were still cleaning up the incited riot the enforcer caused.

"Oh, god. She was there?" Muth said. "I was there the night they took Cynthia. I could've saved her. I could've saved her."

"We're going to find her. Once we do we'll take care of both of you, but you're going to have to give us a ton of information to stay out of prison. You still aided and embedded criminals responsible for attempted trafficking of six young women that we know of."

She hoisted him up and let officers take him, guiding him to safety where he could be processed. Fumero made her way to the exit. She checked her gun, bullets remaining, and replaced the clip with three more shots.

"Where are you going?" Dhavernas asked.

"The Barreling Cask," Fumero replied.

Michaels strode back into the detention center, moving aside for the uniforms bringing Muth out. "Hey, everything okay?"

Dhavernas checked her weapon. "I'm coming too."

"What?" Michaels asked.

"We've got a possible location on the ex-wife," Dhavernas said. "We need someone to watch Muth."

"You go. Don't wait up for me." Michaels shot a thumbs up.

They headed for Dhavernas' SUV, passing by the captain on the way. "Patrols are going to The Barreling Cask. Additional cars assigned to inspect others in the area," the captain said, stooping down to address them through the driver's window before they took off. "Where are you headed?"

"One more life to save tonight," Fumero said. "Then we'll get to work on what Muth knows."

Fumero and Dhavernas sped toward The Barreling Cask. Fumero took the next major step to fracture the trafficking ring she'd been working to destroy.

When they arrived, the place seemed completely emptied.

"Shit, do you think they were tipped off?" Fumero asked.

"There was a shootout at the other bar, it's all over the news and social media," Dhavernas said. "We may have to accept Ellie Sanderson has been moved or we're about to find her dead body."

Fumero nodded. "Let's head in."

They pulled their weapons. As they expected, the front door was closed and locked.

"FBI and DPD, open up," Dhavernas pounded on the door.

They listened for anything. Shuffling, whispering, any indication someone was moving inside. Across the street, people eating at a barbecue restaurant started watching the situation. They continued to eat as they watched the two with their pistols drawn, waiting for an answer.

"No dice," Dhavernas said.

"I'll sweep around the back," Fumero said. "You make sure no one tries coming out here?"

"Patrol is almost here, I'll join you once they arrive," she replied, turning to her radio. "Michaels, how we looking on search warrant? I'm fine using probable cause if we don't have anything."

Fumero walked around the east side of the building. She watched the south end carefully, waiting to see if anyone hightailed it out of the back.

A patrol car approached. They had their lights on. Fumero signaled for them to kill their lights. The patrol car caught on quick, they pulled up on the street next to her.

"There's an FBI agent up front, door is locked and no answer. Relieve the agent. I'm headed in the back entrance, next patrol that arrives have them back us up on the south side. We're waiting on a warrant for entry."

"Copy that," the patrol officer followed orders, driving toward the main entrance without hesitation.

She reached the southeast corner. The tear in her jacket pulled against the abrasive brick wall. Turning, she peaked around the corner. Back door was closed, as were the two, top flaps on the dumpster right by the door itself.

Fumero didn't have a flashlight, so she used her phone. Turning on the app, she threw the first flap up on the dumpster. Peering in, there was nothing but discarded food, paper towels; the usual bar garbage. She tried the door. Locked.

"Dhavernas," she radioed. "Status on warrant? I've got a locked door back here, too."

"On the way," she replied. "Patrol is watching the front."

"Approach from the west, want to make sure there isn't a side entrance or anything," Fumero said.

As she waited, listening for any indications on the other side of the door, a huge black SUV approached. Federal plates. The vehicle came to a stop, and two men got out as Dhavernas arrived.

"They're with me," she replied.

Fumero didn't recognize them. She'd met everyone who worked on the trafficking and Walsh case. It hadn't been long since the Feds took the case away from her.

"New blood?" Fumero asked.

"Local agents, grabbing support from a nearby immigration investigation," Dhavernas replied.

"Did we get the warrant?" Fumero asked.

"Let's get this over with," Dhavernas said.

One of the agents grabbed the handle from the vehicle jack in the trunk and used it to pry the handle off the door. He backed up.

"After you," Dhavernas said.

"DPD and FBI, we're entering the building. If anyone is inside, make yourself known now!" she shouted.

Entering, they cleared the storage area first. Stacks of boxes with paper towels, toilet paper, cleaning materials. To the right, the liquor storage. Stacks of metallic racks held liquor bottles, beer, and keg shells both empty and full. No sign of any hidden closets or doors.

"Ellie Sanderson!" Fumero shouted.

No response.

Dhavernas pointed at the walk-in freezer. "You clear that, I'll move forward."

Fumero opened the walk-in. The cold surge of air came. Inside, the lighting was dim, but bright enough to see a hospital gurney. Empty. The same rig used on the six girls.

Something hit Fumero in the back. The two agents landed on top of her. The first took her pistol. The other put a rag over her mouth, then put duct tape over it, keeping her from screaming. She swung her elbow back, landing on one of the men's ribs. It stalled him, but the other agent kept her from swinging any further. They removed her leather jacket, taking her radio, handcuffs, cell phone and keys.

They used her own handcuffs to secure her to the gurney, locking her right hand onto the gurney frame. They wheeled it out to the dry storage area. As they moved, Dhavernas coldly stared at Fumero.

"I'll handle the cops up front," Dhavernas checked her pistol. "We've got our story locked?"

It all clicked for Fumero. Dhavernas pulled the case from her to let the path go cold. She tried to stifle the investigation. It was why they've controlled the investigation, because Dhavernas was in control of keeping the trafficking organization moving. The one piece of the puzzle she hadn't put together.

Fumero's wrists strained against the handcuffs, the metal cutting into her skin. Her last sight before entering the black SUV was Dhavernas. She screamed for help from the two patrol officers at the front entrance.

The back doors of the SUV closed, silencing her cries.

FOLLOW YOUR HEART
MELISSA KOONS

It was only an hour ago. 4:16pm. Sixty minutes had passed—that was all, but to Daniel it felt longer, much longer. Sixty minutes had stretched into one thousand, four hundred, fifty-two—or so it felt. The clock didn't show the stretched-out moments that elongated into eternity. The analog hands ticked rhythmically as they always did, undisturbed. A few more minutes ticked by, the slamming of the second-hand echoed the passing seconds. How could it be so unaffected by the happenings of a mere seventy-three minutes ago?

Daniel stared across the table at the bedroom door that stood ajar. His large, square hands clasped an old coffee mug; the honeyed tea inside cooling— he had not even taken a sip. He didn't care that it was no longer warm and soothing, or that the honey now clumped at the bottom. His mother drank tea and honey; Audrey's favorite drink was tea and honey, too. He didn't care very much for the beverage, but that didn't stop the women in his life from filling the kitchen with jars and boxes of the stuff. Daniel rubbed his hands along the porcelain of the mug, his wide, hazel eyes remained their unblinking focus on the bedroom door. Daniel studied every contour in the door, every ring, every paint chip. His steady gaze followed the shape, stopping about two thirds down before trailing back to the top to restart their journey.

Daniel looked at the clock— 5:47pm. Daniel tried to remember the lost time of the last one hundred, ninety-six minutes—but couldn't. He searched his mind until he became weary and rested his head on the table. A mental image of the paint chips on the bedroom door rose and lingered in his mind. He needed to fix those. The herbal mixture of leaves and petals wafted up from his mug and tickled his nose. Daniel closed his eyes, inhaling the retched stench deeply. He hated tea.

Daniel watched his mother slowly apply her bright red lipstick. She pushed herself up on her toes and leaned in toward the mirror, tracing her lips delicately— as if she were painting a masterpiece. He stared with fascination at the process. He watched as his mother readied herself for work with the innocent curiosity of a seven-year-old.

"Okay, Danny. Your dad should be home in about twenty minutes so you won't be alone too long." She shoved her feet into her sneakers and tried to smooth out her wrinkled waitress uniform. Daniel watched her silently, his eyes following her as she moved about the trailer hurriedly. She grabbed her purse and slung it over her shoulder. "Bye, Danny." She paused on her way out to pat his head with the affection an owner might have for their dog.

That day, a warm autumn day in September— the 27th of 1983— Daniel saw his mother walk out the screen door at exactly 9:01am. He waited, sitting in front of the door, for his father. Seven hundred, forty-three minutes and thirty-two seconds passed before his mother got home from her job at the diner down the street. His father never came. Daniel counted every second he was alone. He watched the hands on the clock move, slowly ticking away.

"What time did your father leave?" His mother questioned while lighting a Marlboro between her red-painted lips. Daniel looked up at the woman; her shoulder-length, auburn hair pulled back; her flawless skin marred with faint tell-tale signs of age: three lines around her lips, four at the corner of each grey-colored eye, two at the junction of her eyebrows and her nose.

"He never came."

His mother nodded absent mindedly. She took a long drag on the white stick between her lips, pulled the cigarette out of her mouth, and blew the white-gray smoke into the toxic air that surrounded the low-cost subdivision. "Did you just sit there all day, then?" Daniel nodded up at her.

She pursed her lips and shook her head, taking another drag of her cigarette.

He turned away from her, focusing his attention back outside where the crickets chirped in time with the hands of the clock.

"You're a good boy for not getting into any trouble," his mother patted his head and stepped around him. She plopped down on the sofa, snuffing the cigarette out in the ashtray on the coffee table in front of it. Heaving a sigh, she took off her shoes and rubbed her aching feet. "Was I gone very long? There was a huge rush and I had to do a double," she asked offhandedly, her attention focused more on her feet than her son.

Daniel looked back at the small, round clock. Ticking, ticking. 750 minutes and five seconds.

"I'm not sure," he lied.

Daniel raised his head, eyes closed, breathing tranquil. Where was Audrey? They had scheduled a dinner date. Daniel opened his eyes and looked over at the digital clock on the stove: 5:53pm. She should have been home seventy-four minutes ago.

He picked up a discarded spoon and began to methodically stir his cold tea, disrupting the glob of honey that had settled at the bottom of the mug. The click of the metal spoon on the porcelain rim drowned out the hands of the analog clock on the wall. Daniel took a deep breath in and retraced his steps, hoping to trigger the memory of his lost hours. He remembered that he picked up the dry cleaning on his lunch break. His grim eyes shifted to the plastic bags and hangers that he had draped over the back of the couch in the adjoining living room. Sometime in the lost hours they had slid from the back of the couch and slumped to the floor where they bunched up in a clean, wrinkled mess. Those plastic bags never stay put. He remembered that his lunch break had been later than usual—he had a project at work to finish which delayed him. He had to finish touching up the building sketches his boss gave him—silly architects, always concerned more with the big picture; always overlooking the minute details. He would have been allowed to take his usual lunch hour at thirteen seconds past twelve if he had wanted to, but he hated to leave things unfinished.

Where was Audrey? A dull anger burned in his gut. If she made him late for their plans again...Daniel stopped stirring and put the spoon back down on the table instead of in the sink as per usual. Water pooled around the curved metal on the table top, creating a small halo of cold tea. He hated making a mess.

The room shook with the loud music that poured out of the black speakers. Daniel raised the plastic red cup to his lips, sipping the amber colored liquid that sloshed around in it; his intense, grey eyes looking, gazing, studying. He had been standing, awkwardly, at this party for seventy-two minutes and fifty-seven seconds. Fifty-eight. Fifty-nine—

"Hey man! I'm so glad you came!" The host of the party slapped Daniel on the back and gave him a huge, intoxicated grin. "Dude, there's someone I'd like you to meet," he stretched out his arm and pulled a slender woman to his side, a cigarette poised expertly between her index and forefinger, her shoulder length auburn hair fanned out around her face— caught in the momentum of his twirl. "This is my girlfriend, Audrey."

Daniel stared, transfixed by her light blue eyes that shimmered with warmth and were beautifully glazed with intoxication.

"Hey." She greeted nonchalantly, looking over Daniel's shoulder, trying to spot a familiar face.

Daniel stared at her indifferent face in silence, not returning her flippant greeting. She didn't seem to take any notice of his rudeness, her attention was preoccupied with the crowd, instead.

"Jessie!" She squealed and dashed off to greet someone behind him.

Daniel turned, his curious eyes following the woman. He raised his plastic cup to his lips and took a sip, still transfixed on the beauty, his host forgotten.

"Hey—Audrey."

Daniel readjusted the coaster beneath his mug and wrapped his long fingers around the cool, ceramic once more, continuing to contemplate as the ticking of the clock hammered into his skull.

He remembered wanting Chinese. While he was waiting at the dry cleaner's, he phoned Audrey and recommended that they have Chinese for dinner. She said that they should go to the new restaurant; it was nice and required a reservation, which she assured Daniel she would arrange. He just wanted to pick up some Chinese and eat at home, but she wanted to go out so that meant they were going to go out. 6:30pm reservation she had told him. She took the reins on everything. Daniel was used to having to just go along with it. That's what he always did. So, where was she? Daniel looked at the stove clock again: 6:12pm. They were going to be late. Daniel began to unconsciously rock slowly back and forth in his chair. He hated being late.

"Hey, how was your day?" Audrey asked as she shuffled into the living room, a frosted beer in hand. She still wore her work uniform and her speech was slightly slurred already. She plopped down on the sofa across from where Daniel was seated, the newspaper folded into perfect fourths in his hands. The scent of alcohol assaulted his nose as it wafted up from her clothes. This wasn't her first beer of the night. It wasn't even her second judging by the powerful aroma surrounding her.

Daniel looked up at Audrey, his eyes impassive. He set down his paper on the clean, glass, coffee table and stared at the oblivious entity across from him; his steely eyes bearing into her.

"We had reservations for the new Italian restaurant forty-three minutes ago. I called—they gave our table away... twelve minutes ago." Daniel stared, his gaze unwavering.

Audrey looked down, guilt drawn across her face and her blue eyes filled with apologies. She brought the bottle to her red-painted lips. "I'm so sorry Danny," She fidgeted and set her bottle on the flawless table.

Daniel's eyes flickered to the bottle; no coaster, that'll leave a ring.

"I completely spaced," She let out a guilty, frustrated sigh and buried her face in her long, slender hands. "I went out with Janice and the other guys for some drinks after our shift." She buried her face in her hands and groaned.

"We've been together for two years and I can't believe I forgot. You're always giving me reminders, too. I'm so sorry Danny. It won't happen ever again." Audrey looked up at Daniel, her eyes swimming with remorse.

Daniel nodded. He'd heard it all before. Even the guilt in her eyes and regretful expression were common to him. She'd apologized two thousand, five hundred, sixty-eight times over the past two years. It was always the same. It was the same for this: the two thousand, five hundred, sixty-ninth time; and it would be the same for the next: the two thousand, five hundred, seventieth time; too.

188

She was doing it again: forgetting him and their plans. How could Audrey abandon him like this? She liked tormenting him, he knew it. He began to rock faster, the clock a metronome to his pace. Tick, rock forward. Tock, rock back.

Audrey knew how her inability to be punctual bothered him. It was just another one of her manipulations. She couldn't allow him to have any control in their relationship— she had to have all of it. She had to take the reins on everything and he had no choice but to go along with it. Keep his mouth shut and allow the blind to lead him. She didn't know how to navigate her own life, yet she expected him— no, demanded— that he let her navigate his. Demanded that he let her tell him what to do and where to be. Her apologies were all lies. She looked guilty and her eyes shed false tears but she didn't mean any of them; none of the two thousand, five hundred, eighty-three "I'm sorrys" were real. She was just covering her glee at tormenting him.

His mother liked to torment him, that's why she was always late and constantly forgot about him. She did it to weaken him; she took away the rules and deadlines and replaced them with spontaneity and neglect. She took away what he knew so that she would have the power, and he would have nothing to rely on but her. Nothing to gather his bearings. Nothing to give him a leg to stand on. He was at her mercy. The taunting ticking of the clock was a constant reminder of his failure. His failure to keep his promises. His failure to uphold obligations and routine. The failure she made him into. She stole the reins of control over his own life from him, and now Audrey had done the same.

189

Daniel looked up as the screen door flung open and his mother bustled in— nearly tripping over her own feet in her haste. She was pulling at the straps to her dress and her hair was all tousled and mussed.

"I'm so sorry Danny, I got held up at work, and there wasn't a clock," She rambled. Her excuses ambled on as she swung open the fridge door and kitchen cabinets looking for some means of food. She slammed her hands, palms down, onto the counter top and slouched, her spine curling into a defeated posture.

"Looks like I forgot to go shopping again. Sorry Danny, you even made a list and everything."

Daniel's stomach growled. He curled his knees up to his chest and rested his chin on top of them, muffling the sound. He didn't say anything to his mother as she ran her fingers through her hair, her blank eyes wandering over the empty cabinets, trying to figure out what to do next. His stomach growled again and he just closed his eyes. Willing the hunger to pass.

He remembered coming home to drop off the clothes and grab a quick snack, then he went back to work. Audrey had called about the reservation time so he made sure he was home in time to get ready. He looked down at his button-up shirt which was pressed to perfection. The sleeves were unbuttoned and rolled up and the tail had come untucked. His nice slacks were wrinkled, the clean line he had ironed into them gone and disheveled. He despised looking sloppy. .

Daniel looked toward the bedroom door again and his rocking slowed before it ceased entirely. Daniel rubbed the ceramic mug. He had come home and began to get ready for the evening. Daniel's eyes flicked to the plastic bags slumped at the base of the couch. Yes. He'd put them there because he didn't have time to hang them up before returning to work, his suit jacket for the evening was in one of those untouched bags; how he hated wrinkles. His grey eyes slid over to the door again. Daniel started at the top, his eyes taking in every detail— every crevice, and every groove. His eyes circled around the brass door knob and continued his penetrating gaze languidly down.

He had had enough. Too many years half-starved and half-cared for left a hole inside him. A hole that brimmed with anger. It was all her fault. She couldn't control her life and he was done letting her try and control his. Six thousand, two hundred, fifteen days' worth of anger built up inside him like a winter storm. Building and building until his anger gave way and released like an avalanche. Vicious words poured out of Daniel's mouth, pommeling his mother.

"How can you be serious about bringing that incompetent sack of flesh into our home? Into our lives?" Daniel shouted at his mother. Her sleazy boyfriend sneered up at him from the couch but otherwise didn't move—too doped up to pull himself up and give a defense.

Hi mother spun around and placed her fragile hands on her dainty waist.

"It's my life, too Daniel. He makes me happy. If you don't like it, then fine. You're seventeen now, leave! Just like your father." She stomped up to her son, tears dragging black streaks of cheap mascara down her cheeks.

"I don't need you. I never needed you! I tried to give you the best life I could but it was never enough for you. I'll never be good enough for you! It's impossible to meet your standards, Daniel. So go! You do what makes you happy; as for me, I'm going to follow my heart—like I should have done a long time ago before I met your father and got knocked up." She spat in his emotionless face. Her stormy eyes narrowed as she stared, resentfully, at her son.

"I'm going to clean up and when I come out I want you gone." She stormed off towards the bathroom, slamming the door behind her.

Daniel stood rigid. "Fine mother," he growled. "You follow your heart."

Ah, yes, now he remembered everything. His eyes stared serenely transfixed at the bottom of the door. Eight hundred, thirty-four days of anger had built inside him. Eight hundred, thirty-four days of resentment filled the hole his mother had burrowed in his soul. He thought Audrey might be able to mend it, but she only made the hole bigger. Each tear, each missed appointment, each late arrival, and each lie that slipped from her lips stretched the hole bigger and bigger until there wasn't enough to fill him and he felt empty. Only anger had ever filled it. Unlike with his mother, it took significantly less time for his anger to build with Audrey.

Eight hundred, thirty-four days, twelve hours, nineteen minutes. That's how long it took for the storm to silently build inside him. Growing and growing in its silent ferocity. But it wasn't silent when it was released. Oh no. The avalanche of fury Daniel had released was far from quiet—at least for her. There had been screaming, and pleading. Yes, Audrey had indeed begged. Well, Daniel showed her. Yes he did.

A knock sounded at the screen door, jolting Daniel from his thoughts. He looked up and saw a uniformed officer standing on the other side of the aged and filthy screen. He should clean that.

He pushed himself off the couch and stood in front of the officer, not bothering to open the screen door or welcome the man inside. There was no need. He knew why he was here. Daniel's face gave nothing away. He kept his features stoic which matched the calm he felt inside. The avalanche of fury his mother had released in him had long since subsided; the destructive barrage of emotion built up over six thousand, two hundred, fifteen days finally freed and now dormant again.

The office looked him up and down, analyzing, comparing. "You Daniel?" He finally asked.

Daniel nodded, stuffing his hands in his pockets. He had scrubbed them raw to get the motor oil and grease out of the creases in his fingers and beneath the nail beds.

"Is your mother named Annabelle?"

Daniel nodded once more. His heart raced inside him, wishing the officer would just say the words he longed to hear.

"I'm sorry, but I've got some bad news for you, son."

Daniel smiled proudly to himself as he stared at the bloodied scratch marks at the bottom of the door. Audrey's arm limply stretched through the gap. She had tried to run.

He hadn't planned on killing her. It only took four minutes and thirty-nine seconds, but when he saw the bathroom door ajar and her standing there in her chemise and slip carefully applying her bold, red lipstick—exactly the way his mother did: standing on her toes, leaning in toward the mirror, using such precision lost in any other task— he couldn't stop himself.

She had smiled at him when she caught his reflection in the mirror. Daniel smiled back humorlessly, causing her smile to fade. He rigidly meandered toward her. Their eyes maintained intense contact. He had raised his hand and gently began to stroke her expertly curled auburn locks. Audrey leaned into his loving touch, a slight smile returning and turning up her lips, not reaching her steadfast eyes. Daniel quirked his lips briefly before his grip tightened around her silky hair and he slammed her head on the porcelain sink. Her crimson blood flowed down the drain like warm, syrupy water. She had gasped and threw objects at him: the soap dispenser, the toothbrush, her make-up— anything she could grab fast enough. Then she ran.

Daniel had grabbed her arm— the same arm that was stretching for help through the door. She fell. Her feet slid on the carpet, slipping out from under her as he yanked her back. The angel and momentum of her fall broke his grasp, releasing her from his violent hold for a moment. She tried to crawl, her bare knees burned from the carpet. Daniel knelt on the ground behind her, wrinkling his pressed slacks as he shuffled after her until he was within arm's reach. He grasped on to her ankles; her smooth, strong ankles. He pulled her towards him, her slender hands clawed the door and the doorframe trying to stall her capture or use to leverage her way out of his hold. She screamed, blood slid down the left side of her face freely from where it had hit the sink—a chip or porcelain still wedged in the cut. Daniel pinned her legs down and climbed up her until he straddled her, his weight overpowering her flailing limbs.

He had flipped her onto her back and stared into her wide glassy eyes, tears streaming mascara down her cheeks. He claimed her heart and soul. He had the power now, the composure; it was his rules now, his time, his schedule. Daniel stared at her, never flinching as his blue pinstripe shirt became stained with her blood; her cries fell on deaf ears. He had the strength now and she was just a shivering, cowering, mess. No, she could not deny it now. He had finally acquired what he'd been seeking his whole life. He had wrapped his fingers around her pretty little throat, choking the false lies and "I'm sorrys" at the source. He didn't want to hear it. He didn't want to hear it ever again.

He looked back down at the pool of blood surrounding Audrey's body that had soaked into the carpet; that would stain. Daniel tore his eyes away from Audrey's pallid skin to the sink behind him.

He scooted back his chair, the legs scrapped against the laminate flooring with an awful squeak, and came to stand in front of the sink. Yes, he had her confidence now, and he was the only one that could ever have it. He had the source of all the qualities she once possessed; now they belonged to him.

Daniel stared at the organ in the sink, the white porcelain stained with sweet, metallic blood. His mother, after his father left, refused to listen to logic and instead only followed her heart, which got her nowhere and fast. Daniel picked up the muscle, and cradled it in his palms. He smiled lovingly at it and carried it back to the table where he took his seat.

It might as well have been cut from his mother's bosom instead of Audrey's. He had cut the brakes to his mother's car in a fit of rage: just enough that within about five minutes or so of driving time, the cables would snap. Daniel hadn't realized though, at that time in his life when he was seventeen, that all her composure, poise and power would follow her in death. But now, now he rectified his mistake. It was only a matter of time before a uniformed officer came knocking at his door again, bearing bad news that would only uplift his heart. This time he didn't rush to scrub the guilt off his hands. Instead, Daniel placed his treasure in front of him and wrapped his bloodied hands around his mug. The ticking of the clock faded, drowned out by sirens ringing in the distance.

"What does your heart say now, Mother?" Daniel smiled, and raised his cold tea to his lips.

BOOKS BY WRITE ILLUSION

FICTION
Orion's Honor
Dragon Writers
Undercurrents: What Lies Beneath
Shatter Your Image

NON FICTION
Writing a Critical Essay

PORCELAIN PROMPTS
Fiction
Outlining Your Novel
Creating Characters
Heroes
Villains
Conflict and Resolution

Available on Amazon, Barnes & Noble, and major retailors online in both print and eBook formats. Also available on:
www.writeillusion.com
Follow @Write_Koons on Facebook and Instagram

197

GIVE YOUR BOOK THE BACKBONE IT DESERVES.

Spine Press + Post

COMPLETE PUBLISHING & MARKETING SERVICES
FOR AUTHORS & PUBLISHERS.

GET YOUR CUSTOMIZED SOLUTION AT
SPINEPRESSANDPOST.COM

Sign up for our newsletter to be in the latest know of
new book releases at www.spinepressandpost.com
Follow @spine.press.and.post on Facebook and
Instagram

198

Where Everything Goes According to Fan!

Authors Melissa Koons & Thomas A. Fowler dive in weekly to discuss your favorite franchises. You can listen to the podcast for free on all major platforms!

GEEKYGAB.COM

Take a listen and get exclusive blog content at
www.geekygab.com
Follow @geeky.gab.podcast on Facebook and
Instagram

199

A Horror Anthology

www.ingramcontent.com/pod-product-compliance
Lightning Source LLC
Chambersburg PA
CBHW020906180626
46816CB00007BA/2264